DOUBLE NICKELS

ARI SURDOVAL

1

As the last song faded out, the ringing reached from in the house and pulled him down from the sky full of stars. It dragged him back through the tall grass of the black pastures, past the last step of sidewalk and the blocks of vacant lots with Everything Must Go windows, into the chain-link maze of alleyways, over the crabgrass patch of backyard, and up to the rooftop where he sat with his skinny arms on his bent knees. He turned to the jaundiced pall of lamplight that spilled into the dark from his open window and narrowed his eyes.

"Yeah no thanks," he told it. "What time is it even?"

Still he didn't let it ring all the way twice more before he slipped through the window into his small room. The needle lifted at the label. The tone arm swept back and settled into the rest. He crossed the room in a few steps.

He opened the door and stared down the stairs into the dark maw of the hall. The ringing persisted, insisted, relentless, loud now. He held the banister as he walked onto the narrow path into the living room. Reaching to his left, he felt the slits and fissures in the peeling wallpaper until his hand landed on the receiver. He answered the call.

"Hello?" he said into the phone, dreading whatever. A man said he was looking for him with his whole name, Timothy and all, and Tim said, "Yeah this is Tim. This is him. This is me."

The guy started going into the whole thing in these clipped quick sentences like a detective on television. He said, "Take down this location."

Tim said, "Hold on."

He lowered the receiver to the floor by its curled cord and flicked the light switch. The bare bulb scattered shadows over the towers of old clothes and bedding, the trench walls of cardboard boxes that overflowed with old clocks and radios, irons and hairdryers and coffee pots, broken toys and water-stained boardgames, ashtrays and silverware. It was a labyrinth of trash, scavenged from tag sales and Goodwills and the mrsa-ridden mountains of the dump, that teetered like memories from floor to ceiling in ominous precarious piles that crept closer every day.

Tim stepped sideways to where the kitchen table was buried, and pushed aside stacks of faded newspapers and magazines and paperbacks until he found a box full of ballpoint pens. He grabbed one, and an old Time magazine from the top of a stack, and walked back to the phone.

"Where did you say?" he asked.

He cradled the receiver between his neck and shoulder and placed the magazine against the wall beside the phone. He scrawled, Super Stop and Shop Route 22 Jerry Manager, into the fiery clouds of the exploding space shuttle Challenger on the cover.

"Is that it?" Tim asked. The guy said no, actually that's not it, and started getting into it all again.

"Yeah well, like," Tim said. "All right all right. But I don't know how I'm gonna get out there even. I'm in New Miltown. I'm stuck here pretty much. So." The guy started to say something and Tim just hung up.

He knew it was late but it was much later than he thought.

TIM WALKED DOWN THE DARK EMPTY BLOCKS OF MAIN STREET until he ran out of sidewalk, and then he walked in the blue moonlight through the tall grass and gravel on the side of the road. It wasn't September yet but almost and the night was clear. The big Bonanza bus roared past him, headed for wherever, and the breeze felt soft on his face as he walked into it. Up ahead, he could see the moths and June bugs flitting around the lit sign for Buddy's. Past that was just total impenetrable rural darkness.

He sang that last song to himself, imitating the looped operator voice slurring, *"If you need help, if you need help, if you need help, if you need help, please hang up and try again."* From behind him a gray sedan rolled up slow and dimmed its headlights. Tim looked over as it pulled alongside him.

The power window whirred down. From inside a man said, "You look like you need a ride."

Tim clenched his fists in the pockets of his light jacket and looked straight ahead, listening to the quickening of his sneakers' sandblock scratch in the gravel.

"Where's the fire?" the driver asked, slowing to a crawl, inching the car closer to him.

Tim glanced over. He could see half the man's face as he leaned over the passenger seat, one eye closing to see straight, smiling with wet lips to reveal his long ugly adult teeth. He saw the man's hand pat the passenger side of the sedan's bench seat. He saw the thick hair on his wrist as it extended out of his shirt sleeve. He could smell the booze on the guy.

"Get in," the guy said. "I'll give you a ride."

Tim walked faster toward the Buddy's sign and just as he reached it, the bar door flew open with a roar of jukebox guitar. An old bulldog looking guy in carpenter jeans and work boots stumbled out like he'd been spilled, keys in his right hand, his left arm still straight from pushing the door open. He steadied himself with a few quick steps to keep from falling.

From the roadside, Tim called out, "Hey man! Sorry I'm late!"

The guy from the bar looked over and then looked behind him. The sedan pulled away. As Tim jogged across the gravel lot, the guy cocked his head.

When he got closer Tim saw that the guy wasn't old like he looked from far away, maybe not that much older than him even almost. His cheeks were pepper flecked with acne. But his bagged bloodshot eyes looked heavy lidded and his hair was wispy and thinning. His t-shirt and jeans were covered in drywall plaster and construction dust.

"Hey man, sorry," Tim said. "Like sorry to bother you I mean but I'm, like, fucked, pretty much actually? I gotta get to that Stop and Shop, that big new twenty-four hour one out on 22 now and there's like nobody out. You think you could help me maybe?"

The guy swayed like he was hanging from something. The jukebox cried for mercy. It had been waiting for the bus all day. From inside the bar, a hand reached out and pulled the door shut.

"Ha," the guy said. "Nah. You don't wanna be going anywhere with me. I been here for like forever today. I'm going the total other ways anyways."

"Yeah," Tim said. "But like. Seriously? It's kind of like." He looked at the guy and said, "It's just there's nobody else out."

The guy shifted his weight from foot to foot to keep balance. "You got cash for gas?"

Tim looked down. "No?"

"You got any weed?"

"No?"

"You got any smokes at least?"

"No man," Tim said. "I don't have anything."

"Well shit kid," the guy said. "Sucks to be you looks like. Don't it?"

Tim looked down the road at the endless darkness. The guy turned with a long later, drawing out the a, and walked towards a beat up pickup with the windows rolled down. Then, without turning around, the guy yelled, "Oh what the fuck ever come on. I ain't going anywheres anyways I guess."

Tim followed him to the pickup. He reached through the open passenger window and unlocked the door and climbed inside. The guy missed the ignition with the key a couple times. The engine stuttered then caught.

As it shuddered rough to idle, the guy rifled through the ashtray, knocking cigarette butts onto the floor of the cab until he found a short burnt roach. He flicked a lighter and held the long yellow flame close to his face, glowing ghost gaunt and wan in the dark of the cab. He wrestled a weak hit off the speck of spent joint and then ate the tarred bit of rolling paper.

"You go to Wassy?" he asked.

Tim nodded. "Yeah."

"What grade you going in?"

"Nah I'm done."

"Yeah? What'd you like skip or something? You're a little fuckin' little lookin'."

"Yeah just like third pretty much though."

"Oh yeah? You can skip third grade? What're you like good at gluing stuff?"

"I got good at glue later."

The guy snorted, getting it. He leaned against his door, settling into the conversation as Tim shifted anxious and late and looked out at the few cars in the empty parking lot. Maybe somebody else would come out.

"I went there," the guy said.

"Yeah? When did you?"

"A hunnerd years ago. Ha. Nah. Graduated eighty-three?"

Tim stole a glance at his face, surprised he was that young. "Really? Yeah that was like right the year before I started about."

"You play football any?"

"Nah. I didn't really do anything."

"Yeah," the guy said. "I did."

"Oh yeah," Tim said. "I think they got your pictures in the trophy thing?"

"Maybe still yeah."

"What do you do now?"

The guy stared at Tim. "You're fuckin' lookin' at it."

Tim nodded.

"I'm Dan," the guy said.

Tim said, "Hey, Tim."

"You like Maiden?" Dan asked. He pressed eject on the boombox on the bench seat between them and flipped the cassette to the other side.

Tim shrugged. "Nah, not really. I mean, I don't know. Not really."

Dan snorted. "Yeah what're you like a new waver or something? You kinda look like a one."

"I'm not anything," Tim said.

Dan hit the play button on the top of the boombox and shifted the truck into first. The opening riff of The Trooper ricocheted from the cheap speakers. Dan nodded at it and stomped the gas, spitting gravel behind the rear wheels as he pulled onto the road. He swerved into the left lane then swerved back onto the right side of the road and accelerated.

"*This* fuckin' song," he yelled at Tim. When the vocals started, he sang along, looking over at Tim as he drove. Tim looked out the open window as the long stripes of barbed wire vanished against the dark pastures they passed. The metal guitars galloped along like cartoon horses. He rolled his eyes.

2

T he last die of Die With Your Boots On echoed in the cab as Dan swerved into the dark parking lot of the twenty-four hour Super Stop and Shop all the way out on 22. They'd driven the whole album, from side two to side one.

Dan braked and stayed in drive. Tim opened the door and slid off the bench seat. He shut the door and waved through the window. He was about to say hey thanks when Dan pulled away hard enough to make the tires squeal.

Tim watched the truck fishtail onto the empty road and followed the red tail lights until they vanished around a curve. He glanced over and saw the car parked across two spaces in the middle of the empty lot, the left headlight busted and all the windows rolled down. He sighed.

He walked slow with his head down up to automatic doors that yawned open when he got close. He stepped into the pale blue vestibule, with all the carts pressed together like a cage. The bug zapper crackled. He stepped though the second set of doors into the harsh white brightness of the supermarket.

Tim squinted. He took a few steps and looked to his left at the empty checkout lanes, then to his right at the empty produce section. A tinny instrumental Only the Good Die Young cloyed through ceiling speakers as Tim wandered down the empty aisles. He couldn't have said the last time he had been in a supermarket. Maybe the IGA before it closed. This one seemed so endless and empty he felt like he was looking for something in a dream.

And then there she was. Halfway down the cereal aisle, stacking boxes of Lucky Charms that framed her face as she stood on her toes to reach the top shelf. She seemed almost to float above the linoleum.

She had a grown-out crewcut she'd bleached white, the roots dark at her scalp. She wore scuffed black steel-toe safety shoes, like in a factory, with baggy men's suit pants rolled up in cuffs, revealing white tube socks with green stripes bunched at her ankles. The red Stop and Shop apron hung loose around her neck, revealing the edges of a capital X engulfed in white flames on a faded black t-shirt he recognized the second he saw it.

Never in his life had he ever seen anyone who looked anything like her. He couldn't even have made her up but he didn't think she was real almost. Out of nowhere a string quartet played and Only the Good Die Young soared through the store, the cello echoing through the empty quarry he hid in the center of his chest, and the viola as light as his breathing.

When she saw him at the end of the aisle, she put the Lucky Charms on the shelf and stopped stocking. She didn't know who whoever was coming would be, what to expect even. Or if anyone even was coming and what then if they didn't. But she didn't expect anyone like him.

Tim walked towards her slow as if imagining her. She watched him, his shuffling steps, his pants too long, his t-shirt too small, his jacket too big, his hair a mess, his eyes begging like wishing wells. She knew why he was here.

"Hey," Tim said. "Sorry. I'm looking for a friend I guess. Is there a Jerry here maybe? Like a manager? He called me."

"Oh hey," she said. She smiled sad and Tim knew she knew and he wished he could disappear. He wished he'd never heard the ringing. He wished he could vanish into anywhere but right there, caught between her face and her answer.

"Yeah," she said, "they're, he's, Jerry's, in the office. Back there." She motioned to the farthest corner of the store. "You can go back."

Tim looked past her to the end of the aisle.

"It's okay," she said, and then corrected herself. "To go back there I mean."

"Okay," Tim said. "Back there?"

"Yeah like to the right, back past all the meat and stuff," she said. "You gotta go past it. There's a door after."

Tim nodded. And as the aisle pulled him away from her he hoped she wasn't watching him, which she was, over her shoulder as she caught her breath. He didn't look back to see.

He walked along the back wall of the store, past yellow cellophaned chicken, red slabs of beef shrink-wrapped against white styrofoam pooled with cow's blood, stacks of sausage packed like entrails. The meat cases ended at a door with a sign that said Do Not Enter. He pushed it open with his shoulder and stepped into the dark break room.

A wall of red aprons on hooks stood to his right, and to his left hung the time clock and a gray metal rack of time cards. Across the room a closed door leaked light. He stared at it, then turned back to the time clock.

He scanned the names on the top of the time cards, pulling a couple out to check the small box for that Friday night. The first few hadn't been clocked in that day. The next had clocked in that morning and clocked out at five. The next had been clocked in at eight that night and hadn't been clocked out. At the top,

printed in a sure distinctive cursive, was her name. *Cara Sullivan.*
He traced his finger over the clock-ins and clock-outs of the past
two-week pay period. She had worked a lot of double shifts.

"Cara," he whispered.

He tucked the timecard back into its slot and turned to the
door. He walked up to it, hesitated and knocked twice. A
paunchy middle-aged man in a tan button-down shirt threw the
door open. He wore a name tag. It read Jerry Manager.

"Oh okay," Jerry said. "Yeah. Right. Here we go. So glad you
could make it. Gee like, uh." He nodded, agreeing with himself.
"Thanks for coming."

"It took me a while to get here," Tim said.

"Yeah. Yeah it did," Jerry said.

Jerry opened the door to his cluttered office, with the gray
metal desk and the chair with wheels, and the gray dented filing
cabinet, minimum wage and choking victim posters taped to the
white cinder block walls.

And there in the middle of the room, on a brown metal
folding chair, in her patchy fraying leopard print coat with her
arms crossed, and her hair piled up, and her red lipstick lips
pursed into a thin downer scowl, looking like a bag lady, like
some silent film beauty, shaking her head in simmering stage
whisper anger, her huge blue eyes dilated to tiny pinpricks and
locked on Tim, sat Nora.

"Well it's about time," she said, her voice reedy and thin from
pills. "Are you gonna prove I'm me? I told him I was a queen but
he didn't believe me. I said call the president."

Tim took her in and shook his head. "What the fuck mom?"

"What the fuck you, Timothy," she said. "You know how long
I've been locked up in here with this ridiculous little?" She
glared at Jerry. *"Manager."*

Jerry looked between Tim and Nora, as if for sympathy. "I
was trying to help! I was being nice!" He turned to Nora and

pointed. "You know I could have just had you arrested. Arrested!"

"Ooh," Nora shot back. "Arrested! Arrested for what?"

"For what?" Jerry asked. "What do you mean for what? What do you think for what?"

Tim turned to Jerry. "Arrested for what?"

"For shoplifting?" he shouted. "For what. For theft is what."

"Shoplifting?" Tim asked, doubting. He turned to Nora. "Shoplifting? What did you shoplift?"

"I didn't *shoplift* anything."

Jerry sputtered. "Yeah? Okay well here's what." He turned to his desk and pulled open a drawer. "Here's what right here," he said, pulling out several bright colored boxes of condoms and dropping them onto his desk. "And here," he said as he grabbed more. "And here. And oh here's what too." He pointed at the pile. "She was hiding them behind the diapers."

"If you think that's stealing," Nora said. "Wait'll they break your heart."

Jerry shook his head baffled and turned to Tim. "She was wandering the aisles like that all night. I approached her, calmly. Professionally. I approached her nice. I asked if she needed help and she became pretty." He nodded as he searched for the word. "She became unruly. Very unruly. And when I asked her to leave, she refused. That's when I saw her purse was filled with those."

Tim said nothing for a moment. "And then that's when what she like walked out with all that? After she said she wouldn't leave?"

Jerry shook his head, confused. "What? No, she just kept wandering the store, she was—"

"Wait she didn't leave?" Tim asked. He turned to Nora. "Did you leave?"

"Do I look like I left?"

Tim turned to Jerry. This was all bullshit then.

"Okay, well, she's gotta leave with it," Tim explained. "It's not shoplifting unless she leaves with it. You know that though I bet right? Maybe that's why you didn't call the cops actually?"

"Oh I should let her drive off like that?" Jerry sneered. "You know what? Just get out. You get out, and you get out too. Both of you. Don't come back. She's your problem."

———

TIM FOLLOWED NORA DOWN THE BACK AISLE OF THE STOP AND Shop, watching her drag her fingernail over packages of chicken and beef, tearing them open as she passed. As she turned down an aisle to make her way towards the front, she rested her finger on the lid of a jar of peanuts. "Here's what we get," she said, pulling it off the shelf. It hit the tile and shattered.

When Tim reached the aisle, Nora was halfway down, striking a wooden match on the side of a small matchbox, a Kool between her lips. Cara appeared at the end of the aisle with a push broom. Nora lit the cigarette and let the flame burn as she walked, the matchstick curling and blackening until it extinguished in a twist of smoke. Just as Cara passed, Nora dropped the burnt matchstick in front of the broom. She exhaled a gray cloud of menthol that stayed in the air like exhaust.

Tim's face flushed red. Cara saw and clenched the broom handle in sympathy. He couldn't bare to look at her as they closed the distance between them. At the very last moment, he looked up and whispered, "I'm really sorry."

Cara slowed and whispered back. "It's not your fault."

———

In the dark parking lot, Nora leaned against the passenger side of the car, her arms stretched over the hood. She watched Tim cross the lot. She looked up at the night sky. She blew smoke at the moon.

"So just leave me there?" she demanded. "That the plan?"

"The plan?" Tim said. "You have the car. That's the car right there. You're leaning on it. What are you doing all the way out here even?"

"Oh I like this one," she said. "It's a *super* Stop and Shop."

Nora opened the passenger door and got in.

Tim sat behind the wheel and adjusted the rearview mirror. He glanced into it, back at the front of the Stop and Shop. He couldn't see Cara, on the other side of the shopping carts in the dark vestibule, like a wren in a cage, watching him.

Nora handed him the key. Tim turned the ignition and the cranked radio burst on to the pop station, distorting with volume. Madonna sang Borderline. Tim slapped the dial off and turned the key to the useless clicking of the broken starter solenoid.

"Oh this piece of shit," he said. "Of course."

Cara watched as Tim got out of the car holding a heavy screwdriver. He opened the hood and disappeared below it.

Nora sat impatient in the passenger seat, restless, her eyelids heavy. Under the hood, Tim stretched the long shank of the screwdriver across the contact points on the solenoid. He shouted, go.

Nora sat in the passenger seat staring at the empty parking spaces. Tim yelled go again and then hey. Nora leaned over and turned the key in the ignition. Under the hood, the engine block shook to life. A shower of sparks crackled at the contact points. Tim yanked his hand away. He slammed the hood down hard to make the bent latch catch and got back in the car. He stuck the screwdriver under the driver seat.

As he pulled from the parking lot, Nora leaned over and turned the radio back on. She looked out the window as strands of her long hair came loose and blew around her face. The Madonna song was still playing. She sang along. She sounded tired.

3

Cara rolled the rattling blue station wagon through the
stop sign on her corner. She lowered the volume on
the tape in the cassette deck and sang along soft about
somehow rising above it, her heart keeping time as she thought
about that quiet question mark of a kid and told the whole wide
world, in a whisper, to shove it. She pulled in. She listened to the
sparkling guitar and then turned off the car. She sat in silence,
looking up at the yellow light of the kitchen window.

Sitting at the table, between an ashtray and an empty cup,
James studied a passage in a worn blue Alcoholics Anonymous
step book. With a ballpoint pen, he underlined the words,
*"Loved ones, upon whom we heartily depended, were taken from us
by so-called acts of God. Then we became drunkards, and asked God
to stop that. But nothing happened. That was the unkindest cut of all."*
He read the words again and then stared at them, not hearing
the front door close or Cara's footsteps crossing the living room
floorboards.

Cara leaned on the door frame and watched him stare at the
book. "Hey dad."

James looked up. "Oh hey kiddo." He placed the open book

spine up on the table, and then he moved the empty cup, and then he moved the ashtray a few inches.

"What are you doing up still?" she asked.

James nodded to the open book. "Ah, you know. Step stuff."

"Oh they get you going on them right away after I guess."

"Yeah, Tom said to. We did one and he gave me some questions for two."

Cara moved into the kitchen and poured a glass of water from the sink. "What's two?"

James shrugged but repeated it word for word from the placards he had seen propped on tables and taped to walls in church basements for years. "Came to believe a power greater than ourselves could restore us to sanity?"

"Oh yeah?" she said. "It says could?"

"Yeah, could I guess."

"Not will?"

"Well, we'll see how about? How was work though? Which one was tonight, burgers or?"

"No," Cara said. "Stop and Shop again. It was slow. A crazy lady came in."

"Oh yeah?" James asked. "Crazy how?"

"I don't know I guess," Cara said. "Jerry said she was. He made kind of a big deal about it. She was just there a long time walking around pretty much. Talking to herself, singing weird old songs and jingles and stuff. She was pretty messed up."

"Oh," James said. "That's sad. It's tough this thing."

Cara nodded. *This thing.* "Yeah."

Cara set her glass in the sink. James picked up the pen and slid the book a little closer to him.

"Her son had to be the one to come get her I think," Cara said.

James looked up at her. "Oh yeah? Her son you think?" He

looked out the black window but he could only see his reflection. "Geez," he said.

"Tough for him I bet," Cara said, watching him rub the corner of the blue book with the tip of his thumb.

James nodded. "Yeah," he said. "Really tough." He looked up. "But not much longer for you right? Just a couple weeks to go about."

"Sixteen days," Cara said.

"Wow," James said. "Sounds like we're both counting days kinda."

"Yeah," Cara said. "In different directions though."

James let a small soft breath pass between his lips. "Yeah I guess that's right. I wish your mom could see though. She'd be really happy."

Cara opened her hands. She took a breath and thought of her mother, imagined her in the kitchen pouring steaming water over two tea bags in the Red Sox mug. She remembered her standing behind him at the table, her white freckled hands on his shaking shoulders. "She would be," Cara said. "Really happy."

"I don't know what I'm gonna do without you, though," James said. He smiled, trying.

Cara's neck stiffened. "Yeah well, I guess keep reading then. What comes after two?"

"Oh gee I don't know," James said. He picked up the blue book and held it upside down in front him. "I never got that far."

Cara softened and smiled a little. "How was Katy at bedtime? She easier any?"

"I shoulda learned to sing in church when I had the chance," James smiled.

"Oh no," Cara laughed. "Did she make you?"

"Oh yeah. The Cara song."

"No way. Did you?"

"I don't know the words, but," James shrugged. "She can be very persuasive."

Cara tried to imagine it. "Sorry I missed that."

"Yup," James said. He cleared the sudden scratching sadness from his throat. "I'm sorry too."

"Okay," Cara said. "Anyways. Don't stay up all night."

"Me?" James said. "Never. Goodnight. Get some rest. Hey remember I need you to drop me in the morning."

Cara turned in the doorway. "Even Saturday?"

"Yeah. Tomorrow at least. It's the last of the every day ones though. I get the chip."

Cara shrugged.

"The chip," James said. "The coin. For ninety days."

"Oh. Well, that's good dad," she said. She turned back though, before she left the room. Her voice was softer. "Really though," she said. "That's really good."

Cara walked up the stairs and stopped at the small bedroom at the top. The door was cracked. She peered in and the light from the hall fell across her little sister Katy, who had turned ten that summer. She was asleep on her stomach with her ever-longer legs and arms outstretched from under her light blanket.

Cara closed the door to just a crack to let a little light in and walked to her room across the hall. She turned on the lamp on her bedside table and sat on the edge of the bed. She took a watch with no band out of her pocket and put it next to the lamp. She kicked off her heavy shoes and undid the cinched belt and slid out of the suit pants. She tossed them into the corner, on the floor next to the two suitcases that had sat packed for weeks. She laid down exhausted in the X t-shirt she had worked in and her underwear and her socks. She reached out and set her small alarm clock and placed it facing her on the bedside table. She pulled the blanket over her and fell asleep.

NORA CAME THROUGH THE FRONT DOOR SIDEWAYS AND GLIDED
through the towering walls of the maze she had created. She
turned on lamps as she moved through the rooms, each the one
that still lit among dozens. She could have done it blind.

Tim came in a minute later. He never knew where to step. He
always felt like he was about to nudge the first domino. Everything looked like it was about to collapse. Which of course it
had. He felt like he couldn't breathe when he was in the middle
of it all and he imagined soon the door would be blocked and
the windows covered and he'd still be inside.

Nora settled onto the couch in the living room and pulled
her purse into her lap. She cleared a space on the table in front
of her and pulled out two packs of Kools, some lighters, bits of
paper, change and then the pill bottles. Carisoprodol, alprazo-
lam, morphine. The three black horses.

She opened the Soma, the slow cold burn that made pain as
soft as candle wax. It was empty. She shook the bottle of Kadian,
the Kadian that had perched like a raven behind her eyes all
night stretching its long black wings in time release. It was
empty too.

Tim watched invisible. That whole thing with the Stop and
Shop tonight, that felt different. Something was overflowing,
spilling into the world. Or maybe pulling it in, like cold black
seawater. It had always been just a matter of time.

He wondered if he should say that. He wondered what he
would say even or how he would say it or anything anymore
after it had been the way it was always going to be for a while
now. They had passed that, not quite understanding when they
did what passing that meant—how bad bad gets, how fast.
Nobody does.

Nora tried a third empty pill bottle and felt patted by the

rattle of her last two Xanax. She tapped the little green triangles into her hand. She glanced at them against her pale palm, one X up one 3 up, before popping them into her mouth and biting down into the acrid sour powder.

"Such a long night," she said. Not to Tim. Not to anybody. "Such a long, bad night."

She laid back on the old couch, pulling the thin blanket over her legs. She closed her eyes and waited bated for the pills' lying kindness to cradle her.

Tim watched her for a moment, thinking she may say something. After a silent minute, he walked up to his room. He sat on his knees and flipped through the milk crate of records until he found the record that shared, in the strangest way, his name.

He studied it in the yellow script above the painting of the long gray hallway, the sleeve like a message addressed to him. He slipped the record from inside and placed it with care on the turntable. He laid the needle into the empty grooves before the last song on the second side. He loved the soft flutter of the needle floating between songs.

He leaned back against the edge of the bed and listened to the sparse acoustic strumming, the hypnotic chime of the tight capo'ed strings. The singing started. He looked up to the cracked ceiling and watched the singer's parched voice paint the hard days of nothing much at all.

He reached over and tipped back the speaker and slid from beneath it a wallet-sized school photo of third grade Nicky— cow-licked, blonde and smirking—floating in that eternal blue swirl that would always be the background forever. He studied the photograph, holding it by the corners between his thumb and index finger until the song finished.

He placed the photo back beneath the speaker. The needle lifted. The record stopped spinning. He stood. He listened at his door, then crept downstairs to make sure she had not fallen asleep on her back. That had happened a couple times. It was bad. At the foot of the couch, he stood over her. She lay on her side. He watched her shallow breaths and pulled the blanket up to her shoulders. She looked sad.

He turned out all the lamps as he made his way back to his room, holding his breath like he was underwater.

4

—————

Cara watched Katy's face in the mirror as she stretched it still half-asleep. Cheeks puffed, nose scrunched, teeth barred, mouth yawning wide. Cara framed her in the mirror working a handful of tangle with a pink-handled brush.

"Be still," Cara said. She gave Katy's hair a light tug. Katy breathed and met Cara's eyes in the mirror.

"It's Saturday," Katy said.

"Yeah yeah."

"Yeah yeah," Katy repeated. "Yeah yeah."

"It'll be fun. We'll drive around."

"Carvel?"

"You're such a little hustler," Cara said. "No way, ice cream for breakfast."

"That sounds like maybe."

In the driveway, Cara leaned over Katy in the back passenger seat and tugged her seat belt. She didn't like the way the belt fell across her neck and collarbone since her growth spurt, so she had been pretending to buckle it, holding the belt across her so it looked like she was wearing it. Cara had figured it out earlier

that summer, when she was driving down a back road singing
along to some dumb radio song with Katy laughing in the back
seat. She braked hard for a rabbit and Katy crashed through the
space for the arm rest, still laughing. Cara yelled at her after. She
asked, what if we had been going faster?

James opened the passenger door and got in, rolling his
window down and clicking the seat belt in place. Katy said,
"Daddy" in the way she knew he loved, sighing on the first
syllable and letting the second syllable hang in the air for a
moment like a feather. Like she was so surprised, so relieved to
see him.

He was twenty-two when Cara was born. When Katy was
born he was almost thirty. She'd been spared a lot, didn't
remember as much as Cara, wasn't there, was too young to
understand, James knew. But even still, even knowing, the sound
of those two syllables filled him with a feeling like she was
writing to him in the dark with a sparkler. It made it, he didn't
know if easier was the right word, but possible. Maybe really
possible this time. And he would try to recall those sparks as
best he could as he turned himself in the moments that followed
back to the world, into the shame and mistakes that filled the
space between what his daughters had seen and what they
knew.

Cara bumped Katy's door shut with her hip and opened the
driver's door. She got in, nodding at her father, fastened her seat
belt and turned the key in the ignition. She rolled down her
window.

"It wasn't locked," James said.

Cara looked out the window. "Okay. Sorry."

She shifted into reverse and stretched her arm across the
bench seat towards him. She turned and looked out the rear
window as she backed out.

NORA WOKE UP GROGGY, WITH THE RAT SCRATCHING OF withdrawal already starting, scurrying hungry across the length of her shoulders, gnawing at the small of her back. She remembered the Stop and Shop, and the leering sweating Jerry, and Tim and the long ride home, and the way the wind of the open window swept the red sparks of her Kool into the blue moonlit darkness as the radio played.

It's not like she didn't remember. She did. But more and more she'd get mixed up about things. And that would scare her. And out of that confusion and the pangs of fear it triggered and the cold unfolding inevitability of sickness would spring this rage, this automatic mad at the world, the here and the gone, the alive and the dead. The ghosts were everywhere. But only Tim was there.

That morning the thing she got mixed up about was the pill bottles in front of her, empty as strangers' laughter. So when she woke up—god the birds in summer—the guts of her purse spilled on the coffee table, and saw the empty Soma bottle, the empty Kadian and the Xanax empty too, she knew. She knew what she had to know. She knew Tim had taken them after she had fallen asleep. And she knew he hadn't too. But she needed it to be true.

Tim had fallen asleep on his back on the floor in front of the stereo, as he often did, with headphones on. He would never sleep otherwise.

He woke stiff to the sound of Nora pounding on his locked door. He pulled the headphones off as he stretched his arms above his head. He sat. Nora yelled get up, get up, get up as she rapped the door hard with an empty pill bottle.

Tim flipped the lock and opened the door a crack. Nora pushed it open with a slam hard enough to make the door hit the dresser and bounce back so that she had to push it back all the way open. She stood shadowed in the dark doorway, while sun streamed through the bare windows of his bedroom.

She threw the empty bottles at him and missed. They clattered across the floor of his room. "You took my medicine."

"I didn't take your—"

"Bull fucking shit you didn't."

"Your *medicine*," he said.

She smacked him then. That hadn't happened in a while. Like the spilling over he had thought about last night, this was different too. He could hear the fear cutting the anger. This was all going faster now, some accelerator in her, in everything there, had been pressed. He wanted to speak soft, to tell her again he hadn't taken her pills. That worked sometimes.

Of course he had though, not last night but in the past, when the Xanax were still blue, still ovals. When what he had seen flickered on a grainy loop over and over and all the lights on didn't help and all the lights off was even worse, he would sneak one sometimes. When he checked on her, or when she was in the bathroom for an hour. He would press the safety cap open and slide one out if there was enough to slide one out unnoticed, before she started counting, before she had mastered paranoid addict subtraction. He'd break it in half and take it to sleep when it got really bad. But he hadn't at least since the start of the summer, when he caught himself mixing up memories, blurring days into one, getting things out of order. They weren't worth it.

"What do you want me to do?" he said, vague enough for her to take it as a confession or whatever she needed it to be for this to end right this second. And this is how she got him, when she would bend him to pretending. To go along with what they both knew wasn't true. It was easier to just give in, to end the chaos right then, knowing it only made everything worse. In that way, he knew how she felt always. And he knew he knew, and it all tangled together and fell into itself over and over again.

"They just opened," she said. "Go now. Now."

He stooped down and picked a pill bottle from the floor and checked the label.

"Yes," she said. "There *is*. There's one on each." And there was. The typed number one filled the refill indicator box on the corner of the label.

He gathered the three bottles and stuffed them in his pocket. When he looked up, the doorway was empty. He shut the door and locked it. He sat on the edge of his bed and slipped into his sneakers. He went out the window.

———

CARA STEERED INTO THE CHURCH PARKING LOT AND PULLED around the back. She chose a space in the middle of the lot and shifted into park. She watched a few groups of two or three men smoke cigarettes by a back door that was held open with a cinderblock.

"Well that's not very anonymous," Cara said.

James nodded as he undid his seat belt. "Okay okay," he said.

"What's even all the way out here?" Cara asked. "It's too far to go and come back."

"It's just cause it's the Saturday one," he said. He felt bad about it. She could have slept in. But he wanted to pick up the chip, and his sponsor had told him. You gotta pick up the chip. That's part of this. That's important. That's not just for you. Which is how he pushed back the pang of guilt.

"It's just an hour and a half," he tried. "Come a little early. You can meet Tom if you want."

"I do," Katy said, when Cara said nothing.

"Yeah, Beans," he said over the seat. For Mexican Jumping

Beans. Because she couldn't be still. He looked back at her. "Be good."

James got out of the car. He leaned to the passenger window and said, "Ten-thirty?" Cara nodded and watched with the car idling as he walked across the parking lot and fell into the group of men. One offered him a cigarette, another lit it for him.

Cara eased the car to the street. She wondered which way to go and then turned left. It didn't matter much anyway she guessed.

TIM WALKED DOWN THE BACK ALLEYS TO TOWN, PAST THE TRASH cans and chain link backyards. He wondered how he would fill the long nothing of another day but nothing came to him. From behind him a zipping blur of motion whipped past as two ten-year-old boys on BMX bikes bombed down the alley.

Tim gasped and froze. "Hey!" he yelled. His voice cracked. "Slow down!"

The boys shot across the street into the mouth of the next alley. One of the boys leaned back on the seat and turned to look at Tim as he pedaled, raising his middle finger.

"Watch where you're going," Tim shouted.

5

The house rumbled with the thunder of fucked-up adults stumbling to the disco thump of Emotional Rescue. On the porch packed with people, a skinny speed freak looking guy balanced on the front rail and tried to dance, a can of beer in each hand. He stayed up for a moment before losing his balance and landing hard into the tall grass of the front yard. Just as he did, Nora butterflied through the open front door, moving her hips to the beat. Buzzing. Singing along with the lines around her eyes, softer then, when she could still smile wide and wild so her whole face shimmered with something that still shined inside her.

This was back when the house was just a regular shitty house with a couch on the porch and the car out front with the keys in it for whoever wanted to make a run. Before it choked with Nora's hoarding, before all these people flew like sparrows at the first hint of winter, it was the party house. After Buddy's last call for sure, but before too, on afternoons too, on mornings too, when men and women, friends and friends of friends, would drop by speed-eyed or nodding or both or neither even. It was a small town. It was a place to hang out. And weekend nights it was like this, everybody laughing, shouting and rowdy. A Stones record pounding. Nora pushing thirty.

At the top of the narrow stairs, behind the door, Tim and Nicky laid awake in the bed they shared. Tim was twelve still then, Nicky at the end of eight. Nicky could sleep through anything but he was awake, laying on his back and looking over at Tim.

"Why aren't you sleeping?" Tim asked. The bass line rumbled through the floor.

"Because you're not," Nicky said. He rolled over on his back.

"You want me to read that Captain America again?" Tim asked. Nicky shrugged nah.

The door opened with a shock of light and party noise. Tim squinted and Nicky flinched into him, covering his eyes as some man and woman stumbled in.

"In here in here," the guy said. He backed into the room, his hands on the woman's wrists. The woman let herself get pulled in, her tongue licking her front teeth.

Tim sat up fast, with Nicky still as stone at his lap.

"Get out of here!" Tim yelled. "Get out!"

The woman glanced over the man's shoulders to where Tim and Nicky lay frozen in the light like a street kid pieta. "Oh shit there's little kids in here," she said. She pulled the man back by his grip on her wrists. He slammed the door shut behind him and it was dark again and the sounds were muffled. Nicky rolled over on his side, his back to Tim. Tim draped his skinny arm across his little brother's back.

"Get the fuck out," Nicky said in his small scratchy voice, drawing out the u.

"Hey with that," Tim said.

IN THE MORNING THEY PULLED ON THEIR PATCHED JEANS AND sneakers and moved through the passed out bodies all over the living room floor with light soft steps like coydogs. Two men slept opposite each other, arms dangling off the small couch. Next to them a woman snored in the chair. Beer cans lay crushed on the floor, next to empty green bottles stuffed with cigarette butts. The sun came through the kitchen window and grayed in air thick with the sour smell of people breathing out alcohol in their sleep, of drug sweat and the stale incense of weed.

Nicky led them into the kitchen, the countertops and sink stocked deep with empty beer cans and bottles. He opened the fridge door and looked inside with disgust at a couple six pack rings, some packets of fast food ketchup and mustard. Nicky slammed the door shut.

"Nothin'," Nicky said. "Fuck this shit."

"Oh my god what's with this cussing all the time now Nicky," Tim said.

"This is bullshit though," Nicky said.

"Quit. Cussing." Tim whispered. "You're gonna wake up all these assholes."

"Ha ha," Nicky said. "I'm hungry though."

"Yeah well let's get out of here anyway at least."

Tim turned and led Nicky back through the living room to the front door. As they passed the couch, Nicky grabbed the back of Tim's shirt to stop him. When Tim turned back, Nicky was holding his finger to his lips. He pointed to the coffee table, where, between an overflowing conch shell ashtray and some empty bottles, sat a small handheld mirror. And next to the mirror, jutting out from under an empty red pack of Winstons, a rolled up twenty dollar bill.

Nicky reached down and plucked the twenty like it was the

last blackberry in a bramble. He held it up to Tim, with a triumphant grin. Nobody stirred as they made it out.

———

THEY RODE AROUND UNTIL THEY HEARD THE CHURCH BELL SOUND. Before it tolled twice, they turned and pedaled fast, cutting through the empty alleys. They dropped their bikes outside the diner and raced each other to the tall glass front door. Tim got there first and pulled it open, pretending to plunge through and then holding the door open for Nicky.

They stopped in the vestibule by the gumball machines then walked through the second door into the diner. The waitress alone at the register watched them take hesitant steps down the length of the counter and scoot into a front booth lit with morning sun.

Tim leaned over to the tabletop jukebox and flipped the knob on top to read the songs.

"I Love Rock 'N Roll," Tim said. "That one? And Rock This Town. They don't play those anymore."

"You like the fast ones, I like the slow ones," Nicky said. He studied the paper placemat on the tabletop in front of him and tried to decipher the letters that fluttered like hummingbirds around the drawings.

"What's a rag shopper?" he asked. "Oh is it grasshopper? There's a picture of a grasshopper. And a hula lady?"

Tim half listened as he studied all the songs he could play if he'd had a quarter. Nicky ran his finger across a word.

"What's this? All. Danger?" he asked. "Is this ice cream?"

Tim looked over. "Wallbanger. That's drinks. You're looking at the booze menu."

The waitress appeared at the table holding two menus and

glanced between them. "Just you?" she asked. She saw them look between each other, but Tim answered quick.

"We're meeting our grandpa after," he lied. Nicky looked up from the placemat and smiled his smile at the waitress.

"Okay," the waitress said. She placed the menus in front of them. Tim opened his to the breakfast section. Nicky pushed his forward without opening it and turned to the waitress, raising one eyebrow.

"Oh do you already know what you want?" she asked.

"Well let me ask you," Nicky said. He leaned forward as if to share a secret. The waitress smiled and leaned a little closer to him. Tim watched. It was this thing Nicky could do. He just pulled people in. Tim loved to watch it, like a card trick.

Nicky glanced around the empty diner, then nodded to the waitress. "Do you guys make pancakes?" he asked. The waitress laughed.

"Yes," she said, serious. "We do."

"Well I would like pancakes please," Nicky said.

"Okay, can do. Do you want silver dollar or—"

"Oh!" Nicky said. "What's silver dollar?"

"You know," she answered. "Like all the little ones?"

"Oh," Nicky said. "No. I want the regular, the big-sized ones please? And bacon? Is it okay to get bacon too?"

"Sure," the waitress said. "If you want to get the special you can get bacon and sausage and egg too."

"Okay, yeah," Nicky said. "Bacon and sausage. But do I have to get the egg? Can I get no egg? I don't like eggs."

"Yeah," she nodded. "I think that'll be okay." She lowered her voice. "I'll put in a good word for you." She winked at him and he smiled, his face red. She turned to Tim.

"And oh wait," Nicky said. "What are those sandwiches, they have, like, the turkey?" He moved his hand in a little circle over the table. "But where the bread's not together and there's the gravy on it?"

"Open face?" she asked. "Open face turkey sandwich?"

"Yeah!" Nicky said. "Do you make those?"

"Yeah," she said. "Do you want that instead?"

"No and one too please," he said.

"You want pancakes, bacon, sausage, no egg and an open face turkey sandwich?"

"Yes, please."

"What are you?" she asked. "Starvin'?" She jotted down the order in shorthand. "Do you want french fries with the sandwich?"

Nicky paused. "How much for french fries too?"

"They come with it," she said.

"Oh!" Nicky said. "Then heck yeah then. Yes please of course."

The waitress stifled a smile as she wrote it down. She turned to Tim. Tim closed his menu.

"I think yeah, me too please," Tim said. "I'll have that too. The same."

Nicky smiled, proud of himself. "Make it a double!" he said.

———

AFTER THEY HAD EATEN EVERYTHING, AND THE HEAVY DINER plates laid before them streaked with maple syrup and ketchup, and orange pulp stuck to the sides of the red plastic juice glasses, the waitress approached. She tore the check from the top of the book and placed it face down in front of Nicky. "There you go hon. No rush." Nicky sat up straight in the booth, trying to look as big as he felt.

Nicky flipped the check over and read it to Tim. "Sixty-one

fifty!" he said, worried. Tim tilted his head at Nicky and took the check.

"*Sixteen* fifty," he said.

Tim fished the twenty from his pocket. He unrolled it and flattened it against the table as the waitress watched with a look of concern. Tim placed it on the table on top of the check and it rolled up again. He straightened it and set it flat on the table, weighting it under a salt shaker.

Nicky nodded. "Keep the change!"

———

TOO FULL, THEY PEDALED THEIR BIKES SLOW THROUGH THE EMPTY Sunday morning streets of town. As they rode past the church, its bleached white steeple gleaming against the blue sky, Tim looked down and saw Nicky's shoe lace loose and dangling close to the dirty unguarded chain. Tim slowed.

"Hey wait," he said.

Tim laid his bike down and kneeled at Nicky's feet, double knotting the lace. Across the street, the doors of the church opened and pastel families streamed out. All yellows and pinks and blues in store-bought clothes like new, the shiny brown shoes they put pennies in. The congratulated sons had their collars popped and the protected daughters' dresses were smooth as paper.

Tim and Nicky watched like they had tumbled from a dust bowl, smelling like the diner's fryer but not in a full way anymore, just greasy now, just dirty, just stolen. Tim tugged the loose chain of Nicky's bike to make sure it stayed threaded on the flywheel. He wiped his fingers on the back of his jeans as he stood, looking at the kids their age across the street.

They coasted down the road unnoticed and pedaled to the back way to the falls. They ditched their bikes and hiked the trail to the top, the roar of rushing water hushing them till they got to the point where the white capped rapids crashed over the slick dark rocks and cascaded into the first of a series of deep pools, staggered like steps one under the next. They sat quiet, together.

Tim gathered a small handful of pebbles and walked to the edge, tossing them one at a time into the water.

"Make a wish," Nicky said.

"That's pennies," Tim said.

Nicky watched his brother and wondered something he didn't want to ask again. "Do you think dad is really gonna send a Pac Man?" he said.

Tim looked over as if refusing to answer. "No." He shook his head at the idea even.

Their dad. Never answering. Not at that number any longer. Number disconnected. Calling whenever. In the middle of the night. One time when they were supposed to be in school. The sounds of people in the background, music. Lying his face off, Tim thought, while Nicky pressed his head against his to share the phone, to hear too and worse, believe.

"Do you think he's ever going to come back?" Nicky asked over the shush of the falls.

"No," Tim said. "He's not."

"Is California far?" Nicky asked.

"California?" Tim said. "It's about three thousand miles." He lifted both middle fingers toward the rolling green hills of the horizon. "That way. If that's where he is even."

"Well maybe he would," Nicky offered. "If it got bad enough?"

"Yeah what to make it twice as worse?" Tim asked. "I wish he was twice as gone."

Tim turned and sat back next to Nicky. He leaned back but

the grass to the side of the trail was still cool with dew in the shade of the tall trees. He sat up and hugged his knees.

"Do you really don't remember?" he asked Nicky. "You can't just. You can't like, hold on to thinking he's gonna come back somebody else and make everything all like the church people."

Nicky nodded, pretending to accept it. "What about us though?"

Tim looked down the winding path they had climbed. "Who?"

Nicky's breaths grew jagged but Tim didn't notice until Nicky said, "That's not funny," taking a short quick breath between each word.

Tim turned back and leaned into Nicky, their shoulders touching.

"Nah c'mon," Tim said. "We're just gonna go to school till we're done and then get out of here."

"But you skipped!" Nicky said. "You're gonna be going in ninth *early* when I'm not even in fifth *yet*. You're not gonna be there even when I like lose the ticket or anything and when I, when I like, when they." Nicky struggled for a breath as he fought to keep his head above the flash floods of worry that rose in him.

"Hey, hey," Tim said. "It's okay, it's—"

"And then what do I do when you go when it's just me? What's like, gonna, how's, when I, when, like?" Nicky lost his thought in the rapids of the worry, his voice thin and tight.

"Nicky. Nicky." Tim said, nudging him again. "Over here. Over here." He held up his index finger. "Make a wish."

Nicky pulled in a deep, stuttering breath and exhaled in a soft trickle against Tim's fingertip like he was blowing out a candle.

"That's pennies," Nicky said, his voice settled.

"Candles too," Tim said. They sat quiet, listening to the waterfall.

"But really though," Nicky said. "What am I gonna do when it's just me?"

"What just you?" Tim said. "It's not ever gonna be just you, I keep telling you." Tim said.

"Yeah," Nicky said. "That's what everybody says."

"Oh you think I'm everybody now?" Tim said. "You think *I'm* everybody?" He picked up a rock at his side and leaned back. The sun behind him, he aimed at the horizon and threw it as hard as he could. He looked at Nicky, who didn't answer.

Tim shook his head. "And stop hiding the ticket in your desk all the time. Just put it in your pocket and don't take it out every ten seconds. I told you like a hunnerd times. You're always checking to make sure something you already know you have is still there. That's how you lose everything."

They sat there for a while and then walked down the steep wooded path back to their bikes. They rode side by side, taking the longest way home. When the country back roads turned to streets with sidewalks, they rode into an alley.

Nicky was pedaling easy, his arms swaying at his sides, when the chain slipped off. He grabbed the handle bars and dropped his feet, dragging his sneakers to stop. He looked down at the chain dangling off the flywheel as Tim circled back.

Nicky straddled the bike, holding it by the handlebars while Tim knelt and threaded the dirty chain over the teeth of the flywheel. He guided it to the rear sprocket, leaving thick grease streaks on his fingers. He lifted the back wheel by the frame and fitted the chain back on. He turned the pedal with his hand and the back wheel spun.

Nicky rode in a small tight circle. "Race to the end?" he asked.

"Ready set go," Tim said. He picked up his bike.

"Don't let me win," Nicky said. He took off down the alley.

Tim hopped on his bike and pedaled fast enough to catch up.

"You better hurry," he called out. "I'm right behind you!"

Nicky leaned forward and pumped his short legs like pistons against the pedals.

"You better go!" Tim yelled after him.

They raced the last length of the alley, Nicky in the lead. He glanced fast over his shoulder to make sure Tim was pedaling hard, to make sure he was winning for real. He grinned into the wind, close to flying, not seeing Tim coast after he faced back forward. As the street approached, Nicky slammed back on his pedal to brake, fishtailing the bike into a hard, sharp stop. He held his arms up in victory.

Tim shook his head as he pulled up next to him. "You're too fast!" Tim said. "I like blinked and you were gone."

They rolled their bikes to the end of the alley, out of breath. Tim looked both ways down the empty street and Nicky followed him into the next alley. They got smaller as they rode away, Tim swerving in slow swoops by shifting his weight from side to side.

Nicky pedaled with his hands on his thighs and then twirled them in little disco circles as he sang in an exaggerated English accent. "I will be your knight in shining *ahhhhh-muhhhh.*" He tried to sing the rest but he cracked up laughing as they rode into the shadows.

6

The pharmacy opened at nine on Saturdays. Tim walked in a few minutes after to the ring of the bell above the door. Another empty store, he thought. He stopped and watched the watches rotate in the Timex display case, then walked to the back counter, passing the hot rod model kits and the greeting cards and the hairsprays.

The pharmacist walked through the swinging doors that separated the room where he counted out the pills. He saw Tim standing at the counter with the empty bottles and frowned.

"Are there really refills this time?" the pharmacist asked.

Tim slid the bottles toward him. "One," he said. "It's typed."

"If I get one more phone call," the pharmacist said.

"She knows."

The pharmacist checked the refill indicators on each of the labels. "Come back before noon."

Tim walked back to the front and thought, when's it now, though? He stopped again at the display case full of watches, but each face showed a different time.

CARA DROVE AWAY FROM THE CHURCH, NOT SURE WHERE TO GO. Katy cupped her hands to the sides of her mouth and whispered from the back seat, "Carvel."

Cara laughed. She pulled a white cassette from the center console and pushed it into the tape player. The marching drone of The Unheard Music faded. Cara reached forward and turned up the volume as the tape spooled between songs. In the second of silence, Katy said, "Yes."

Two sharp snare sparks lit bottle rockets of electric guitar double stops that shot from the speakers and burst out the windows onto the sunny empty road. Cara and Katy moved to the music, major to minor, slamming laughing against the seatbelts. Cara sang along as loud as she could. She howled the lyrics at the windshield and everything past it. And then, at her part, singing with the man's voice, Katy joined in and screamed with her.

It was a singalong. They did it all the time. It was one of Cara's favorites, which made Katy love it too, and they sang the chorus together as Cara drove. *"The world's a mess it's in my kiss. The world's a mess it's in my kiss. The world's a mess it's in my kiss. The world's a mess it's in my kiss."*

And at the next stop sign, Cara thought why not and turned to where she was pretty sure there used to be a Carvel, down the road a little ways.

———————

TIM WALKED DOWN THE SIDE OF THE ROAD, ABOUT A HALF MILE away from the pharmacy and thought, come back before noon I hate that guy. He could have just filled it. There was nobody there even.

He heard the music first. And again, he thought maybe he was imagining things, because X was coming out of nowhere loud and getting louder. Then the blue station wagon emerged over the ridge ahead of him.

Inside Cara laughed as Katy smacked her lips in kisses in the rearview while they sang. As they drove slow past where Tim stood stunned, Cara was looking in the mirror at Katy and yelling the chorus so loud her voice cracked. Katy sang along with her. *The world's a mess it's in my kiss. The world's a mess it's in my kiss.* Then she turned and blew a kiss out the window right at Tim as they passed, with Cara laughing so hard she didn't even see him.

Tim froze. That was her. That was the girl. That was the same girl right there. And he turned and watched the car drive towards town, the music getting softer as it drove away.

"No," Tim said. "Way." And he started back to where he had just come from as fast as he could walk.

KATY GRINNED AT CARA IN THE REARVIEW MIRROR AS THEY PULLED into the Carvel parking lot. "No way is yes," she said.

"Looks like it," Cara said. She opened Katy's door and they walked together to the slanted glass front, the giant model vanilla soft serve cone leaning like it would topple from the roof. Cara held the door open for Katy and they walked in.

Behind the counter, Darcie was surprised. She had just then unlocked the door and flipped the sign to welcome. She was wearing the blue, square bottomed shirt with the white collar, and after her second warning that summer, the stupid white visor with the Carvel logo across the front. Her hair, home permed into tight curls crisped shiny with hairspray, rose like plumage from the visor, and fell below her shoulders with long streaks of boxed highlights. It came out okay, she thought. She felt stupid in the uniform, but at least it wasn't a cap. And it was almost September. Maybe she could find something better after summer. It was already slower. No one wanted ice cream in winter.

"Hey," Darcie said as Cara and Katy walked in.

"Hey," Cara said. Katy pressed against the counter and looked at the menu on the wall above the soft serve machines.

"Fudgie the *whale*," Katy read.

"You would," Cara said. "You want a cup or a dipped?"

"Ooh dipped," Katy said.

Cara smiled at Darcie. "Hey can we please get two vanilla chocolate dippeds?"

"Yeah totally, let me just check they're coming out good. Just opened."

Darcie turned and grabbed a small styrofoam cup and pulled the lever of the vanilla soft serve. A glob of ice cream fell into the cup. Darcie sniffed it and tossed it into the trash. "Yeah it's good."

She held a cone under the soft serve spigot and pulled the handle forward like a slot machine. She moved the cone in small, precise circles and layered the thick stream of ice cream onto it. With perfect balance, she walked a few steps to the well of chocolate topping. She tapped the side to make sure it had heated up. She lifted the lid and plunged the vanilla ice cream up to the cone into the watery chocolate topping and pulled it out fast. She let a few drops of topping fall and then turned the cone right side up as it hardened into a shell. She turned and handed it to Cara, smiling as Katy followed it with her eyes wide. Darcie did it again and handed the second cone to Katy.

The grin on Katy's face made Darcie smile, her face bright as a spotlight, her dark Italian eyes squinting almost closed with kindness. "She's cute," she said.

Darcie stepped over to the register and rang them up, and as she did, Cara noticed all the bracelets on her wrist, handwoven and colorful, some faded, some bright. Kind of hippie kind of metal but it would be cool to do that, to get good at it. She could make them with Katy before she left and each have a special one.

"Three bucks," Darcie said. Cara handed her a five, and as Darcie pulled two singles out of the drawer, waved her hand.

"No no, that's cool," Cara said.

Darcie smiled. "Oh right on," she said. "Thank you. Nobody ever tips."

"Believe me," Cara said. "I know."

———

TIM'S HEART LEAPT AND FELL WHEN HE SAW THE BLUE STATION wagon parked in front of the Carvel. As he had walked back fast, his thoughts blooming with hope, he answered himself, there's no way. There's just no way. But he kept walking and then he saw it and god of all places.

Cara and Katy walked out holding their cones and Tim stopped and watched thinking should he run, to her before she drove away, or off the edge of the world if she did. And then they turned and sat down on the metal bench in front of the Carvel, and he felt a deep rush of relief, a glowing ember of a maybe. He forced his legs forward, walking slow to come up with anything to say.

But he couldn't. He couldn't think of anything to say that wouldn't be a lie. And he already had a thousand of those. His steps got slower as his brain raced. He got closer.

Cara had her back turned, wiping ice cream off Katy's chin and cheeks. Katy watched Tim walk those last few steps like he was in slow motion. She stared at him when he stopped.

"Hey," Tim said to Cara's back. "Hey. Sorry. Thanks. I just, I wanted to say like hey and sorry. And thanks." He winced. Cara

heard him and turned, confused, looking up into the sun to
see him.

"Hey, I just wanted to say like hey and sorry and thanks
again," Tim said.

"What?" Cara said, bothered. "Again?" She blocked the sun
with her other hand.

She saw him right as he said, "You're the girl. From Stop and
Shop? From last night?" And it was him, it was that kid. "You
were at Stop and Shop last night. I had to come in?" It was him.

"Oh," Cara said, caught off guard. Katy, so used to the under-
current of determination in her sister's voice, looked over,
surprised. "Yeah," Cara said. "Yeah, hey. Woah."

Cara stood up, excited and nervous and took a step forward
as she did. Too close, she took a step back and took him in. "How
are you doing? Are you from here?"

"Oh nowhere," Tim answered. "I mean, nothing. Yeah pretty
much. Not too far."

"Where'd you go?" Cara asked.

"Just Wassy," he said.

"Oh yeah," Cara said. "I think we played you. What year are
you?"

"None," he said. "I'm done." Cara figured he must have
meant he dropped out. He looked young. Lots of kids did it. You
could get your license and drive over and drop out on the
same day.

He didn't know what to say next and he looked over at Katy
who stared at them both with curiosity. Cara glanced back and
saw the circle of ice cream around Katy's open mouth and
handed her one of the napkins that she had started holding
tighter.

"That's Katy," Cara said. She turned to Tim. She said, "I'm,"
and Tim bit his bottom lip to stop himself from blurting it with
her, "Cara."

He was so glad to have a reason to know the name he had been tracing behind his eyes since he saw her timecard. He said it back to her. "Cara. Hey."

Inside, Darcie saw Cara stand and talk to someone, and walked around the counter to look. When she saw Tim, she stopped and felt that lonely reaching feeling he gave her. "Oh," she said. "Look at you go, Tim." She watched him through the window, his hands in his pockets and his head down sheepish, facing Cara.

Through his reflection, Tim saw Darcie turn and walk back towards the counter, out of sight, and he felt sorry. He turned back to Cara and the silence felt like how he had imagined falling from someplace very high would feel. He had been keeping to himself for a long time now. It was hard to talk sometimes.

Cara could tell. And then she remembered him turning out of the aisle while she held a box of cereal hoping he would turn around. And she thought of how dark the breakroom always is, and how he had to walk through it alone having never been there and she remembered that being dragged feeling of having to deal with things like that. And she remembered that look he had as he walked away and it was like the look her mom sometimes had when things got bad. Just the look of doing it anyway. And she imagined that he had turned around last night and she had been able to tell him all those things before he had to go alone back there. She imagined she'd told him she knew how that felt. But the moment that she stood and imagined it just felt like silence to Tim, alone in front of her in the bright morning sun.

He backed up. "So," he said and he reached for the words that could tell her that there were times in summer but winter too when he would be on the roof staring at the sky and it would be the middle of the night and it would be so clear with so many stars out that it almost wouldn't look like nighttime but it wouldn't look like day either. It looked like this other kind of time where the dead of night glowed with a kind of light that burned bright even though it was gone and he'd breathe so slow he could almost float and that was the same feeling he had when he saw her last night and that was the feeling he felt right now. But what words said that?

"So," he said again. "I like saw you so I wanted to say hey. And, you know, thank you. And sorry."

Cara nodded, thinking, better to just let it go, and said, "Okay. Cool. Thanks." She didn't sound like she felt, but he was turning back anyway and it was August already. She looked down at her hand, covered in melted chocolate and ice cream. Embarrassed she turned for the napkins on the bench.

Tim took a couple steps back and gave her a small shy wave. He said, "Okay." He turned to leave.

"Hey," Cara said, still holding the cone. "Wait what's your name even?"

"Tim," he said. Surprised, he tried not to smile.

"Tim what?" she said.

"Essup," he told her. "Like mess up without the m."

"Is that your punk rock name?" she asked.

"Ha," he said. He smiled. "Nah. I wish I had a punk rock name."

"You kinda don't need one," Cara said. She smiled. "Thanks for saying hey," she said.

"Yeah?" Tim said. Everything she said sounded like hello and goodbye at the same time. "Well. Thanks for. I don't know." He shrugged.

"Nothin'?" Cara flirted. Tim's heart stuttered.

"I almost said everything," he said.

"Same diff," she quipped. She made him laugh.

He glanced at the blue station wagon, and turned back to Cara and said, "X is awesome. By the way. I love them."

Cara gasped. "Oh no!" she said. She laughed. "Did you see that?" She shook her head. He had seen them, alone how they really were, her and Katy when she felt most free and real, and he knew that song and loved it too. She stepped closer to him.

"It was so cool," Tim said. He smiled at Katy. "She knew all the words. Like a little Exene!"

Cara clutched her hands in prayer. "Exene," she sighed. "I love her. With the old dresses and all the bracelets? Like on the back of Wild Gift?" She looked over at Katy. "She's John Doe on that actually."

Tim nodded, happy, "Yeah she is! I used to like try to comb my hair like on that, that picture of John Doe, like where's he's building the house of cards? Like back kind of?"

"Oh yeah?" Cara nodded, glancing up at his uncombed hair. "You weren't always all Tommy Stinson'ed out?"

Tim shook his head amazed. "How'd you even know that?"

Cara fell into his eyes in the parking lot, in the sun, smiling, shining like a new penny. "I'm on to you," she said.

7

I n the church basement, dark enough even with the morning light coming through the street-level windows at the ceiling to require the overhead lights to be on, James sat on a brown metal folding chair. He didn't sit in the circle—the chairs arranged at the center of the room—but in the second row of chairs outside the circle. Not in the back though, and in the first chair so he could stand up and not have to walk over anybody when they called the times.

In the center, in front of one placard that listed the 12 Steps of Alcoholics Anonymous and another that listed the 12 Traditions of Alcoholics Anonymous and cardboard signs that read "One Day at a Time" and "Easy Does It" and "Let Go Let God," among the people who sat in the circle to be sure they would talk, always, Tom held court.

Sharing his experience, strength and hope, James thought. He was trying to accept the words, to speak in the phrases they said would make this stop somehow, which it had. For longer than it had in a long time already. It is why he had chosen Tom to be his sponsor right away this time, to learn how to talk and think in the ways that would make it work.

Tom was fluent, and he wove his fluency with threads of hard-won understanding and no-nonsense tenacity, with flourishes of seeming self-effacing humility that he always pulled back like the last act of an illusion to reveal, out of thin air, his insights.

James looked up at laughter, realizing he hadn't been listening, as Tom smoothed back his hair and gave a perfected head shake.

"Same damn thing," Tom said. "And that's what I thought you people were gonna tell me too. The same. Damn. Thing. Now see I've been around for a few twenty-four hours now. But when I was in my first twenty-four, my real first, my last first, for today right? I was sitting in one of these very chairs here, at this same meeting, and I was looking around, thinking—*thinking,* right? Thinking, what are these people telling these things for?" He glanced around the circle to give a beat. "That's private!"

Hummed laughter murmured from the other men filling the chairs. *Private.* Nervous, James smiled along. Tom continued.

"And I was sitting there, with my arms crossed, reading all you, thinking you people were just *nuts.* There was no way you could help me. Hell, I had a little advice for all of you, in fact."

Tom paused and nodded at the small laughter, pleased. "See, that was my best thinking. And my best thinking got me right into one of these chairs, ass first I might add. That's Tom working Tom's program. But see I was waiting for you to come kick me out! Eighty-six me from the rooms! 'Cause, you see? That's where this disease takes us. We think we're better than and worse than—at the same time. At the same time? Now that's insanity. The very definition of it: Thinking two opposite ways about the same thing at the same time."

There were some nods of agreement from the men. James glanced around the room. He knew he would never be able to not do that.

Across the circle from Tom, a man watching time held up a small red stop sign with the word "Time" printed on it.

"Thank you," Tom said to the man with the sign, charging ahead. "But here's what an old old timer told me after my first meeting. Came up to me, when I was sitting with my arms crossed, hiding shakes, and here is what he said. He said, Boy, you *stink*."

Several men laughed.

"You smell terrible he said," Tom said. "So when you meet me tomorrow morning, take a shower first. I'll be at the nine-o-clock over in New Miltown. And you know what? I did. Whiteknuckled it and met him here the next day. And I took that shower first. First suggestion I ever took. And when that old timer—it was Walt, and I know a lot of you remember him—walked in, I remember being real happy to see him. That was the first person I'd been happy to see in a long time. And when he saw me, he said, 'Nice to see you.' Like we were walking in the park. And that's the first time I'd heard that in a long time too."

The time keeper held up the stop sign again. Tom nodded and continued. "So the first suggestion I ever followed was the second suggestion too and the one I follow every day and the one I'm following right now. Same damn thing. It's keep coming back."

James leaned forward and placed his elbows on his knees. He couldn't imagine ever being able to talk for as long as Tom talked.

"Because this ain't a program for people who need it," Tom said. "I wish it was. I truly do. It's a program for people who want it. You see people come in all the time and sometimes you can just tell, just by looking at 'em, they still got years of fucking up ahead of 'em. And I'll tell 'em. Rigorous honesty. So like the Big Book says, 'If you want what we have to offer, and you're ready to take certain steps?' Well for me those steps before we even get to the real steps mean my footsteps, walking through that door, no matter what. So if you're new, remember, we all been new. Some of us been new quite a few times. But it's about showing up. Showing up, no matter what. So keep coming back. And keep coming back. And keep coming back. Just for today."

———

TIM WALKED CARA AND KATY TO THE BLUE STATION WAGON. CARA shut Katy's door behind her. Tim stood a few steps away as Cara got in the car and turned the key in the ignition. She leaned out the window and looked at him.

"Hey, so what's the best way to kill an hour around here?" Cara asked. "I have to pick up my dad in a while."

"Where is he?" Tim asked.

"He's at like a meeting," Cara said.

"Oh I meant like where is he where do you have to get him?" Tim said. "Where is his office?"

"Pretty close," Cara said.

"Oh I would just go to the falls then," Tim said.

"Oh that big waterfall?" Cara said.

"Yeah, it's beautiful," Tim said. "It's the best. I used to go all the time with my little, like when I was little I mean."

"How do you get there?" Cara asked.

"Just keep going pretty much," Tim said. "It's like right there. Haven't you ever been?"

"No," Cara said. "I heard about it."

"How could anybody grow up like anywhere around here and never go to the falls?" he asked.

"I was busy," she said.

"I guess you were, yeah," he said.

Cara looked back at Katy in the rearview mirror and then

looked over at Tim. "You wanna show us how to get there?" she asked.

"Sure," he said. "It's like right there."

"Yeah you said that," she said. She smiled, looking at him.

"So yeah so," Tim said. He tried to focus. "Just go like—"

"No," Cara said, "I mean do you want to show us?"

"Oh, like," Tim said, his throat tight. "Like right now?"

"Yeah," Cara said.

"Like go with you?"

"Uh, yeah," Cara said. "Like go with me. Us. Are you busy?"

"Ha," Tim said. "I'm never busy."

"You're lucky," Cara said. "So okay then. Get in."

"Okay," Tim said. Cara watched him.

"Okay," she said. She leaned over the long bench seat and lifted the lock on the passenger door. She sat back behind the wheel and looked over at him. "Now's good."

Inside the Carvel, Darcie watched Tim walk around the front of the car and get in. As Cara backed out of the space and pulled onto the road, Darcie watched. "Whatever Tim," she said.

———

THE SOFT-SPOKEN, OLDER MAN WHO CHAIRED THE MEETING PLACED a tackle box on his lap. "John again, still an alcoholic," he said. "Thank you all for a great meeting. I've asked Bob to give out the chips."

He handed the tackle box to the man to his right, who opened it to reveal the aluminum coins arranged by color inside. "Thank you, John," Bob said. "My name is Bob and I am an alcoholic." Several men said hello to him.

"Here at the Saturday Morning Second Chancers group, we have a chip system to acknowledge sobriety. The chips are not a reward or a guarantee. They are a recognition of continuous sobriety in the hopes of carrying the message to the new comer that this way of life works, one day at a time. The first chip is red for thirty days."

He held up a red AA coin. "Red like a stop sign," Bob said. "Thirty days? Anybody have thirty days?" He placed the coin back in the tackle box. He held up a yellow coin. "Next we have yellow for sixty days. Anybody feeling yellow? Don't be scared!" Bob looked around the room. "No takers. How about green for ninety days? Green light. Maybe still a little green around the gills. Would anybody like to celebrate ninety days of continuous sobriety?"

James raised his hand. "I have ninety days today," he said. As he stood from the chair, the room burst into applause. James turned bright red and shook his head. Several men cheered and yelled his name. His throat got tight as he walked into the circle and Bob stepped to him.

Bob handed James the green ninety day chip and hugged him. James hugged him back. Somebody shouted, "How'd ya do it?" And then several other men shouted it as well. James stood in the center of the circle and looked down at the chip. There was a three inside a circle inside a triangle. Above the triangle, it read, To thine own self be true. On the other side was inscribed the Serenity Prayer. He rubbed the raised words of the prayer with his thumb and shook his head. "I don't know," he said. "Not alone, that's for sure. Not alone."

———

WHEN THE MEETING CLOSED, JAMES STOOD IN A CIRCLE WITH BOTH arms across the shoulders of the men next to him, and their arms around his.

"Thank you all for a good meeting," John said. "James, would you like to take us out?"

It was nice to be asked, James reminded himself as the men looked over and the hot flush rose into his cheeks. He knew what he was supposed to do. He swallowed and nodded, pushing back memories of scowling towering priests, of welted palms and prayers said wrong, of first days, of the dull flash of red then black from his father's backhand, of you fell down, of the crash of dishes swept from the table, of the hot fog of Four Roses and Old Golds inches from his mouth making him cough as his father pinned him against the refrigerator with the question, the question and the answer. *You got a problem? You got a problem? I'll give you a problem.*

God he hated this part. But what does hating something even mean when there's no other choice anymore? He said what he was supposed to say.

"Who's in charge?" James asked the group of men. And, together to answer, they all said "God" and recited The Lord's Prayer. James said it too. He had to.

They folded their chairs and carried them to a closet in the hall. They filed out the back door and stood in small groups in the church parking lot. James stood by the door and accepted the congratulations with small genuine thank you's. He watched Tom make his way from group to group, chatting before walking over to him.

"James lad," Tom said. "Ninety days imagine that. In a row no less."

"Yeah," James said. "Feels good."

"It will pass," Tom said.

"Oh," James said. "Yeah. I guess it will, yeah."

"The good feelings pass, the bad ones pass," Tom said. "They all pass. Everything passes."

"Okay," James said, nodding to show he would be sure to remember.

"How's that second step coming?" Tom said. James brightened.

"Oh, it's good. I finished. I finished last night. I got Katy to bed and then read it through again and sat up and—"

"Well alright," Tom said. "When do you want to work it?"

"Oh, whenever you want," James said. "That'd be great."

"Well then how about now?" Tom said. "I've got a few things at the house I could use a hand with. You can get a little service in too."

James looked away as the other men splintered off and walked alone to their cars. "Now?" he said. "I would, but, it's just."

Tom allowed the silence to hang between them. "Big plans?" he said.

"No, no," James said. "It's just that, you know, Cara's got Katy and she's coming any minute to pick me up. She has to work later, and I'm still not allowed to drive yet, so I gotta—I can't apply for the limited permit until a hundred and twenty days, so I still have to—"

"Okay, okay," Tom said. He held his hands up as if to surrender. "Uncle." Tom shook his head in mock wonder. "Nobody can give a longer answer to a yes or no question than we can. No problem. I just wanted to offer up my Saturday morning. That's what this is about. Doing for others. That's the spiritual foundation. That's what gets us out of me."

James nodded. "I understand," he said. "I'm really sorry. I want to. She's just had Katy all morning, and it's her only morning off practically, and—"

"Yeah, yeah. I got it, I got it," Tom said. "But James. You understand, anything you place in front of your recovery you're going to lose. Right? That's not me saying that. That's how this disease works. Cunning. Baffling. Powerful."

James nodded again. "I do. I really do. Understand. Can I call you later to work out a time?"

"Of course," Tom said.

James looked down at his feet and then looked up again. "Should I still be, you know, calling every day?" he said. "Now that I got ninety?"

Again Tom wielded the uncomfortable silence. "Well," he said. "I guess that's up to you. Use your best judgment." James nodded, not sure what the answer was. Tom could tell and seemed to weigh that as some type of indication."You call whenever you think you should, James."

"Okay," James said. "Thanks, Tom. Really. I don't know how I would have done this so far without you."

Tom looked pleased. "That's what we do," he said. "It's I got drunk, we get sober. That's how it works. It's a we program."

"Got it," James said. "Got it."

"Well," Tom said. "We never *get it*. Congratulations on your ninety."

"Thanks," James said. He leaned forward to hug Tom but he was already turning away. Tom turned back and hugged James with one arm and a nod. He walked away.

James watched the last men leave the parking lot. He leaned against the side of the church and waited for Cara.

8

Tim led Cara and Katy away from the car and into a meadow of wildflowers, kicking up mayflies as they moved through the tall grass. As they approached a dark line of trees, Tim turned to Cara with Katy between them and said, "Oh this is the back."

"Sneaking into the waterfall?" Cara asked.

Tim smiled a little and said yeah. "It's right through there," he said. Cara watched him step into the cool shade of ash trees.

Cara put her hand on Katy's shoulder as they stepped out of the sun. They followed Tim. A few paces in she could hear the soft call of the water. It grew louder with each step until the trail opened into a clearing.

They stepped together into the sun, a few paces behind Tim. Cara blinked till she could see the cascade of water roaring over the rocks high above them and crashing into the large pool of water at the base across the clearing. Tim led them to the edge. The waterfall cascaded in front of them and the water of the pool was so clear Cara could see the white rocks at the bottom shining in the sun like little moons.

"It really is the back," Tim said. He pointed through the

curtain of water. "That's the park right there on the other side, where the parking lot is? You can get up here through that trail, but it's a little steep so most people just stay over there."

Tim motioned towards a path along the side of the pool. Behind them, the trail climbed steep with slivers of sunlight seeping between tree trunks mottled with moss, up to the top where he'd go with Nicky.

Cara sat on a flat warm rock that looked down on the pool and watched Tim walk Katy to the water's edge to show her the crayfish. He held her hand so she could lean over the clear water. She turned back and yelled up to Cara. "We found one!"

Tim walked back and sat beside Cara. They sat quiet while Tim watched Katy. He hadn't been here for a long time.

"I can't believe this is here," Cara said. Tim looked over at her.

"I know," he said. "You don't ever expect to find something so cool right in the middle of where you've always been."

"How'd you find up here?" she asked. Tim tried to remember the first time he had ever been to this spot.

"Wow," he said. "I don't know. It's like when did you first ever hear the Beatles?"

"When did I what?" she asked, confused.

"First ever hear the Beatles," he said. "Like it's just always existed. But I don't know. I guess my mom must have brought me when I was little. But, really little, it must have been. Before I could remember."

Cara hesitated, looking over at him. "Has she always been like that, like how she was last night?" she asked. Tim pulled up a long blade of grass and tied it into a knot, and then tied another knot over that one, thinking of how to answer. "You don't have to talk about it," she said. She thought it wasn't fair to ask him.

"No, it's alright," Tim said. "No she hasn't been like that

always. But she's always been something I guess. It's not just one thing. She was trying kinda, for a while. Then, I don't know. Everything changed all of a sudden."

"That must be really hard," Cara said.

Tim shrugged. He wanted to say that things are only hard when they don't last. When it's forever, it's just the way things are. "You get used to it," he said instead. But that wasn't it.

"It's like you know when you wake up in the dark?" he said. "And you can't see anything and you don't know if you're dreaming or awake but then you start to be able to see and everything is still there all the same and the dream goes away? And you're like oh yeah. Or you know like, the opposite? Like when you walk out of the movies in the day and you can't see cause it's so bright. And you almost feel like you're someone in the movie still then all of a sudden everything is back to what's real again. Like both ways you get used to it I mean."

"Uh, *okay?*" Cara said. She didn't like how she sounded.

Tim looked away, silent. "I don't know," he said. He didn't really understand it himself. "Sorry. Never mind. Sometimes I can't explain things in ways that everybody gets."

Cara looked over at him. She was angry at herself for asking. Because now she had to pretend to be someone who didn't understand. And she knew she didn't have to do that with him. He screamed she didn't have to do that with him as he sat there so quiet and jagged and soft. But she did. She just wanted so bad to stay there, right there, for just a little bit just like this, just with him and not everything else too. Everything that ruins everything.

"Oh yeah?" she asked. "You think I'm everybody?"

The question surprised him. He wondered where he had heard it before. But before he could get lost in trying to remember, her face held him still, right there next to her, like the pull of gravity.

"No," he said, his voice quiet. He looked at her and she looked back at him. "Maybe I don't think I do."

She nodded once. "Good. Cause I'm not."

He looked down between his knees and smiled. "That's cool," he said. He shrugged and looked right at her, trying to do that thing Nicky would do. "You know, most people are."

Cara's eyes smiled full of light, loving that. "Most people are everybody?" she asked.

Tim shook his head. "Yeah, they really are."

"They *really* are," Cara said.

They watched Katy walk away from the water and pick a handful of dandelions. Tim turned to Cara. "So like what do your parents do?"

Cara looked away. She could almost make out the shape of families on the other side of the waterfall. "Oh you know, just like regular parents stuff. Totally normal family, like a TV show practically. My dad works and my mom like, makes cookies or whatever."

"Wow cookies?" Tim said. "Really? That sounds kinda nice actually."

"Yeah, it is I guess," Cara said, like she imagined a girl like that would talk. "It's boring I guess but, yeah, she's awesome."

"That really cool," Tim said. "And your dad does just like business stuff you said?"

"Yeah totally," Cara said. She watched Katy place the heads of the dandelions on the surface of the water. The undertow pulled them out toward the rocks.

"Like at an office?" he asked. "Is that where you have to pick him up?"

Cara iced with dread. "Oh *shit*," she said. "What time is it?" Tim had no idea. Cara jammed her hand in her pocket and pulled out the watch. "Oh shit it's 11:30 almost. Oh god I'm so late." And then Tim remembered the pharmacy with a stab of panic. It closed at noon like a nightmare until Monday. "I gotta go too," he said. "Can you drop me off back over where I was?"

"If we hurry," Cara said. She scrambled to her feet and called to Katy. She cupped her mouth to her hands and called her name again and Katy looked up. Cara yelled hurry. We have to hurry.

In the car, Cara and Katy were both silent. No music played. Cara's knuckles whitened tight on the wheel. Tim looked at her hands.

"Is he not cool about stuff like that?" he asked.

Cara shook her head and mouthed the word no. "He is not," she said.

9

Nora moved in small circles through the paths of the living room and kitchen, holding on to herself, flinching her elbows into her ribs with each shock of withdrawal. She sat when her heart raced but when her legs started kicking like she was dreaming she was falling, she stood. And as she did she seemed to be watching herself through air blue from Kools. Her teeth burned as if they were dissolving and she pinched them to be sure they were there.

She stood at the front window and lit a cigarette. She worked through the time again in her head. They opened at nine even if he walked slow where did he even go what did he even do anymore even if he went somewhere he would have gotten there by half past. How long could it take to fill them it's morning it's a fifteen minute walk where could he go? He should *be* here. He should be *here.* She looked out the window at the empty street feeling like she was falling down a set of endless stairs. Standing still, plummeting. Somewhere there was a box of broken alarm clocks and it sounded like they were all ringing. Between her fingers the long ash of the Kool burned down to the filter.

Cara stopped past the Carvel and put the car in park. She turned to Tim, her foot on the brake, ready to put it back in drive. "I'm sorry," she said. "I have to go right now. Thank you for showing us there. I'm so glad you walked by. I'm so happy you said hi to me."

Tim unbuckled his seat belt. He turned over his left shoulder and smiled at Katy as he opened the door. Katy smiled back. He leaned down to the open passenger door window. "Would it be okay if I like?" He stumbled over the question.

"I have to go, I'm sorry," Cara said and pulled the car into drive.

Tim nodded and stood. "Okay."

Cara shook the steering wheel and mouthed a silent scream. "Wait, wait," she said. "I have to leave. I have to leave but—"

"I know. I'm sorry. Sorry you do I mean," Tim said. Then he plunged forward, in this last possible moment. "Can I see you again?" he said. "Can I see you any sometime?"

Cara shook her head. She was so late.

"Just say yes?" Tim said. "Please just say yes?"

"Shit!" Cara said. "I just—yes. Yes." She took a breath. "Yes."

Tim smiled, shocked. She said yes.

"Yes," Cara said. And she steeled herself and she didn't care she was late. She slowed. "Yes please."

"Yes," Tim said. "How?"

"I don't know," Cara said. "I always work."

Dan had half a last beer still a little cold between his legs nursing it driving around waiting for Buddy's to open when he saw Tim get out of the car and lean down to talk to Cara. He thought hey there's that kid again, and he turned up the boombox on the seat next to him. He leaned out the window as he got closer, blaring metal.

But even slowing down and smacking his palm against the outside of the driver side door to the double kick guitar hysterics, Tim didn't look up. He didn't even notice. Dan slammed on the brakes as he got alongside Cara and threw horns with his left hand as he leaned out the window and banged his head in time to the music.

Katy jumped against her seatbelt in the back seat and Cara spun around mid sentence. Dan pushed in the clutch and stomped the gas pedal, smoking the back tires. Tim threw his hands in the air.

Cara turned back to Tim, shaking her head. "I have to go," she yelled over the screech of the tires, the sour cloud of burning rubber billowing through their windows. She lurched the car into the street and drove off. Dan popped the truck into gear and took off in the other direction. Tim stood there, alone, the air full of smoke and the stench of burned rubber. He watched Cara speed away. He cursed, then cursed again, then sprinted toward the pharmacy.

AS SOON AS SHE PULLED INTO THE CHURCH PARKING LOT, CARA saw James. He sat on the steps of the church and watched her as she pulled up. He stayed seated and stared at her for a moment, as Cara looked forward through the windshield. Katy leaned out the window and said, "Hi daddy."

James stood and walked to the passenger side. He got in, shut the door, buckled his seat belt, all without talking. He looked over at Cara. She stared straight ahead.

"Do you know what time it is?" he asked.

"Yes," she said.

"So you know how late you are?" he asked.

"Yes," she said. "I just."

"You just what?" he said. Cara didn't answer. "You what?" he said.

"Me nothing," Cara said. "I just got lost."

"Lost where?" James said.

"Nowhere," Cara said. "Driving around. Singing. We got lost a little." She glanced at Katy in the rearview mirror. Katy looked at the reflection of Cara's eyes.

"Okay, well," James said. He searched at a loss through words he hated for something he could say. "Maybe for the next, say, sixteen day—oh, wait, sorry, fifteen days now right? Maybe for the next fifteen days you could help me out a little? Be where you say you are going to—"

Cara spun and faced him and the sting in her eyes as piercing as her mother's stopped him before she could even interrupt. "Help you out a little? A *little*? For the next *fifteen* days?" She stared through the window and said, almost in a whisper, nodding, "Help you out a little."

James looked out his window and imagined he was being lifted off somewhere by balloons he held tight but the balloons were his daughters. He felt Katy staring at him. What could he say even? He looked through the windshield at the parking lot. He looked at where he was.

"It's about showing up, Cara," he said. "It's about showing up no matter what." He felt empty as his words. He shook his head. "Just go."

———

TIM TURNED DOWN THE ALLEY WALKING FAST, THE PILL BOTTLES rattling like maracas in his pocket with every other step. He crossed the patch of grass in the back and pulled himself up onto the roof and through his open bedroom window.

When he walked into the living room, Nora was curled on

the couch, knees to her chest. Her blanket didn't cover her bruised legs and she stared at a cigarette burning in the ashtray. Her arms felt so heavy. She felt so tired. And there he was all of a sudden, standing in the room. Had he been here the whole time? Why would he do that? She pulled herself up to sit and reached for the bottles of pills.

"I'm sorry," Tim said. "He made me wait until he closed."

Nora pushed with great effort at the top of a bottle but couldn't open it. She handed it to him. Tim opened it and gave it back, saying nothing. She tapped four Xanax into her palm.

"Wait," Tim said. "That's the green ones."

Nora shook her head. Said the little detective, she thought. Said the upstairs ghost, she thought. She put the pills in her mouth and laid down, chewing them frowning. They tasted so bitter. She closed her eyes and waited for them to kick in.

———

ON THE ROOF OUTSIDE THE WINDOW, TIM SAT IN THE SUN. He looked down the alley, and the alley after that, and the next. And he thought about Cara, and he couldn't believe all that happened and he couldn't believe that guy and that then she drove off like that. And he thought of her face when she said yes then yes please. To him. He thought if he thought about her any harder she might hear him.

10

Mick was on the yellow Triumph that night when he pulled into the parking lot of Buddy's, the bike shaking and spraying oil behind him. He spotted Nora's car in the lot as he veered in. It was hard to miss. Even in the miserable early March wet snow, in the middle of the night, with a flickering headlight, coming down.

He killed the engine and kicked down the stand. He was straddling the bike pulling off his gloves when he heard Refugee bleeding through the walls of the bar. He could just see her in there now. He stuffed the gloves into his red Woolrich jacket pocket and pulled the bottom down to be sure it covered his waist. He unfastened the white speckled Bell helmet and pulled it off his head. He cinched the chin strap and walked into the bar carrying it.

It wasn't that crowded for a Friday night but the stools at the bar were full. People stood holding bottles and glasses, talking, resting their drinks on the table top Pac Man, leaning on the pinball machine next to the jukebox as the guitars and organ blared. Mick stood in the doorway looking from face to face for hers.

The bartender was ringing someone up, facing the register and didn't see him come in. And all the way down the bar, Bennetts, the bouncer, didn't see him either. He leaned his thick left forearm on the bar, facing away from the room. Bennetts was so big, all Nora saw from behind him was the wall of his black jacket, his hulking chest, his beer wet mustache, his nicotine teeth, the RORER 714 stamped on the quaalude between his thick thumb and index finger as he held it out to her.

Nobody saw Mick but Tim.

Sitting next to Nora on the last seat at the bar, his head just above the cups of cut lime and lemon wedges and the bar mats, Tim tied knots in one of the stems of all the maraschino cherries they had eaten. He picked the last cherry from the double rocks glass and dipped his head below the bar. On the floor at the foot of Tim's barstool, Nicky slept, the blue jacket Tim had outgrown rolled up under his head, Nora's leopard print coat his blanket.

Tim held the cherry down and said, "You want the last one?" Nicky took soft breaths and didn't stir. Tim sat up and yawned. He popped the cherry into his mouth and held it between his teeth. He pulled off the stem and dropped it into the ashtray with the others. That's when he saw Mick in the doorway, staring at him with a look of sadness and disgust.

"That's *dad*," Tim whispered. He reached over slow under the bar as Mick watched and tugged Nora's shirt hard and said too soft to hear, "That's dad right there. That's dad."

Nora pulled away. As the bartender passed, Bennetts moved his finger over the two empty rocks glasses in front of him and Nora. The bartender filled both with well bourbon. Tim pulled the bottom of Nora's shirt again and she jerked forward. "Stop pulling me back," she said.

Mick watched from the doorway as Nora took a drag of her cigarette and put the quaalude on her tongue. In one fluid motion, she knocked back the pill with the double shot and set the rocks glass down in front of her and exhaled a slow billow of smoke.

Bennetts laughed, his brown tooth smile pushing his big red cheeks out. "You forgot to say cheers!" he said.

He had always liked her, the way she piled her hair up on her head looking pretty without trying and how she didn't care what you didn't like, the way her eyes could lock on you like you were the only person. One cold slow night she snuck up behind him at the door and listened as he sang along to Cowboy Song, just quiet to himself. She bumped into him from behind and when he bowed up and turned she said, "You have such a pretty voice Bennetts." It was sweet she thought, how red he went, swallowing hard, fumbling for words. "Oh," he said. He shook his head embarrassed and laughed at himself. "I didn't know you were right there." She stared at him for a moment and said, "What is your story, Bennetts? You're not just gigantic are you." And she seemed to really want to know, as if she could be a friend to him. One time, later, after his sister Sara got sick, he had stopped by to drop off some groceries and check on her. As he was coming out, Nora was walking up with a bag of groceries too. She was just like that.

Tim caught his eye and Bennetts smiled at him. "You wanna play some more pinball my man?" he asked. He slid four quarters towards Tim, his wide happy face boozy and beaming. Such a cool little kid. Quiet. Polite. He put a thick hand on Nora's bare forearm as he leaned forward. "We got Space Invaders."

Bennetts turned to point to the video game at the other end of the bar and that's when he saw Mick, and Nora saw Mick, and Tim said, again, but resigned this time, "That's *dad*. That's dad right *there*."

Bennetts stood and turned, his jacket rising black as a tornado on the other side of Nora. He sighed, "goddammit."

Mick moved down the bar, clenching the helmet by the strap in his right fist, glaring at Nora with dark angry eyes.

Tim ducked down under the bar and said, "Nicky, dad's *here. Dad's* here." But Nicky slept. Tim sat up as Mick rounded the bar shouting at Nora, "Why though? Just why?" Nora cocked her head at Mick and smiled. He yelled it again. "Just why?"

A few people looked up and over, but the bar was full enough and the music was loud enough that under the glow of the little color television playing the time to make the donuts commercial with the sound off, nobody even looked up yet. They just looked into their drinks and leaned towards each other to talk.

"What are you even doing?" Mick asked.

Nora rolled her eyes, pinned and high. "I'm doing whatever I want," she said. She leaned around from behind Bennetts, protected. "You fucking hitting me bullshit piece of shit *motherfucker*, I'm doing whatever I want. That's what I'm doing."

"You're crazy now," Mick shouted, loud enough that the volume of the bar ebbed to notice. He maintained an arm's length space from Bennetts, and Nora behind him, as if repelled by the negative attraction of a magnet from getting any closer. "Where is Nicky?" he shouted.

"He's right there," Nora said, and pointed towards the floor.

"Nora!" Mick cried, with true worry. "He's sleeping there? Look at Tim!"

Pale and trembling on the barstool, Tim's eyes cut between his father yelling and his mother's back as Bennetts stepped between them.

"Okay not in here man," Bennetts said. "Not in here."

Nora glanced over her shoulder at Tim and turned back to Mick. "Gee he was fine a minute ago. I wonder what happened?" Nora said.

Mick stood stunned, staring at the unseeable force that like an undertow pulled her further away every day. Everything was going wrong. It wasn't supposed to be like this. None of this was supposed to be like this.

"You know what happened?" she asked. "*You* happened. You're what happened. You're what happens to everybody."

Mick turned to Tim. "Tim, get Nicky. Now. Let's go." Tim froze. What did let's go mean?

"Yeah you gonna put em on the bike?" Nora smirked. And Mick knew she was right and he stood there coiling tighter, knowing, with Bennetts looming over him, trying to be reasonable, Mick's thin sharp face level with the center of his chest.

"You're all fucked up look at you," Mick said, angry and aching, and then turned back to Tim. "Get Nicky now, Tim, please now," he shouted, his eyes burning. He could take Nicky first, have Tim wait outside and then come back. It wasn't far.

The bartender looked over at Bennetts. Bennetts held up his hand to say he'd take care of it. Around the corner of the bar, a few people stood and moved away. The air seemed to thin and dry with electricity.

Bennetts stepped forward and put his hand on Mick's pigeon chest. "Come on man," Bennetts said, his voice even. And then kinder, trying to diffuse. "Do yourself a favor for once."

Bennetts put a slight pressure on Mick's chest with his big open palm and Mick pushed forward against his hand. He looked at Nora, "You're all fucking fucked up, look at you," he pleaded.

Nora laughed. "*I* am."

Mick yelled, "Why?" Just to all of it, why?

Nora glared at him standing there asking that here. "Because fuck you that's why," she said, burning with fuck it inside. Fuck it, fuck the whole shortchange lie. "Fuck you forever. Mick. You *talker.*"

"Okay," Bennetts said. "Time's up." He pushed forward with

a few steady steps, moving Mick backwards like a plow. Mick looked at him for the first time, as if just noticing him.

"Get your hands off me," Mick said. He pushed Bennetts' hand off with his forearm. "Mind your own business."

"This is my job," Bennetts said, stepping forward.

"Yeah this is your job," Mick said. "I saw you working both jobs there. Both jobs huh?"

Bennetts shook his head and said, "Last time I ask."

In a long moment, they faced each other. Then, fast, Bennetts grabbed Mick's left arm and spun him around towards the door, trying to get a bouncer hold on his left elbow and wrist.

Mick wrestled his arm loose and turned back to Nora, as if to say something, but then turned to Tim. "Get Nicky!" he shouted.

Bennetts pulled him back around, lifting Mick's red Woolrich jacket for a second as he did. Tim glimpsed the black handle of Mick's Charter Arms .38 Special revolver tucked into the back of his dark jeans. He'd seen it on the table once. He knew where he kept it.

Tim slid off the barstool and stood stiff as Bennetts pushed Mick forward by the shoulder from behind. Rather than pushing back against him, Mick grabbed Bennetts by the wrist and rushed forward, pulling Bennetts off balance. He opened his grip on Bennett's wrist as he felt Bennetts stumble. A pace ahead of him, Mick spun back and swung the white speckled helmet full force into Bennetts' nose and mouth.

Bennetts' stunned face snapped back, arcing a thick rope of blood from his nose and split lips, his front teeth shattered by the blow. He stumbled back waving his arms to balance, knocking over a small table as he went down, splattering glasses and bottles around him.

As people jumped up, Tim dropped below the bar and threw himself over Nicky. "Tim?" Nicky asked as he woke. Tim rolled off him and pulled Nicky's head to his chest and protected it with both arms, said don't look don't look. At Nora's feet, holding onto his little brother so he couldn't see, he looked up at Mick yelling at him, yelling, "Get Nicky!"

Past him, Tim watched Bennetts stand, holding a thick glass beer stein by the handle in his right fist. Bennetts yanked Mick around and punched him full force to the side of his left eyebrow, the beer stein exploding in shards of glass as it connected.

Mick landed deadweight hard on the floor right in front of Tim. His face looked half masked. The right side was untouched, but his left cheek caved in. His eyebrow dangled almost severed and drooped in a thick bloody peel over his bulging crooked eye. The large shards of broken glass sparkled in the cut pink skin and the white exposed bone glowed under the dark slick of blood that poured from it. Tim gagged but he couldn't take a breath, couldn't do anything but hold Nicky tight against him so he wouldn't see. On the jukebox, the singer's thin cold voice sneered something about someone getting kicked around some.

Mick blinked his eye, dazed, trying to see, while he pushed confused at the thick flap of ripped skin that covered the other. He reached towards Tim as Bennetts stumbled forward with heavy steps and reared his boot back to kick. Mick felt the steps coming. He lurched up. He grabbed Bennetts' left ankle and mule kicked back against the knee. Bennetts screamed and collapsed as his knee cracked back.

Before Bennetts could sit up, Mick was on top of him. With Bennetts' throat in his left hand, he rained punches down into his face with his right fist, just letting it all out on him, every sharp dull sting shooting up through his wrist another why.

When it felt like he broke his ring finger, he reached back, and pulled the gun from the small of his back and pistol-whipped Bennetts across the cheek, asking why again, and then once again, thinking this is what happens, this is what happens when you care. Bennetts didn't move, couldn't even raise his hands to cover himself. Mick stopped, out of breath and covered in blood, straddling Bennetts' chest.

Unmoved on her barstool, Nora looked down at them on the floor. She turned back to the bar. She picked up Bennetts' full double bourbon and shot it back.

Thinking he saw something out of his left eye, Mick stood and pointed the pistol at the bartender who held up his hands. "Get away from me," Mick said. He turned to the people who had crowded at the end of the bar and raised the pistol at them. "Get away from me."

He looked at Nora and shook his head in sadness and then kneeled in front of Tim. "Tim hey look it's okay," he said, his eye socket shattered, his eye floating crooked as it swelled. "It's okay. It's okay."

Tim shook his head and said, "No no no." Nicky had gone limp against him, knew he didn't want to see, knew to trust Tim. And the guitar on the jukebox was screaming a bent note and Tim heard the mountain of Bennetts on the floor make a gurgling noise, the fingers that just pushed the quarters towards him, palm up and twitching.

Mick reached out with his smashed right fist, blood covered and knuckle cut, broken finger bent and swollen, and tried to tuck Tim's hair behind his ear, then touched his cheek and said, "It's okay." He tried to smile. There was blood on his teeth.

And then everything fell into darkness, everything but Nicky in his arms and Mick's twisted, ripped faced covered in blood saying, "It's okay. It's okay." And Tim closed his eyes and listened to the echo of himself saying, no, no, no.

And on the floor of his bedroom, Tim repeated no as he woke slow, as if floating to the surface of the recurring nightmare. The droning guitar of Refugee got softer and Mick's face fell away until it was just Tim, clenching Nicky quiet in his arms. And then Nicky was gone too.

Tim laid there, awake and alone, with the memory pressed against him, pushing him back, as if to say, okay, time's up. Last time I ask.

11

Tim stayed quiet in his room for a while, listening for Nora. When he was sure he didn't hear her, he opened the window. He climbed out onto the roof and laid over the edge on his stomach, craning his neck to the front of the house. The car wasn't parked out front.

Back in his room, he turned in circles, looking for something he wasn't sure what, wishing he could find it in there. In the days since he'd last seen Cara his chest seemed to swell and crest with hope and loneliness. On the roof or on the floor, he played things she said over and over like songs, her face and her hands in his head like scenes from a movie, and he wondered how he could see her for real again.

He flipped through his records, looking, considering. He thought he could make her a mix tape. But he didn't have a blank tape. And he didn't have any money. He could tape over one, but. He didn't know. He flipped through his records again, and then sat still by the record player for a while.

He opened his locked door and stared down the stairs at the reaching heaps of Nora's hoarding. All that after just a couple few years. In some ways it made it easier to think of everything out there as just one massive thing, something impenetrable. It wasn't though, and it scared him to know that because to him it meant he understood it. Or knew her in some way he didn't want to know her ever, when he wished he'd never met her. The trails through the sprawl led like threads of thought, like tangled reasons in a lost language he could somehow read. Her lonely angry autobiography written in ten cent treasure and trash.

He descended into it. To get to the other side of the table, he had to crawl under it. He shimmied on his stomach through a tunnel made of paperbacks and cardboard boxes full of whatever to the other side. Past there, in the corner, between towering piles of more loose open boxes set a delicate deco lamp of a small bronze woman naked on jagged rocks, in her outstretched arms the white globe that held the bulb.

Tim knelt and switched on the lamp. He pushed aside a large box of old photographs and pulled towards him one of the boxes of old records. There were many. Nora had her own, but she had also inherited two large record collections from friends. One overdosed. One killed herself.

Most were from the sixties, all the usual ones but others too. Ones he hadn't expected when he first found them, before they formed the walls of this little shrine under the dirty window and everything grew around them. He opened another box and flipped through it until he found what he realized he was looking for. The Beatles in blue and black, arms outstretched, together and apart. Help!

He flipped it over and looked at the songs listed on the back. Help! You've Got to Hide Your Love Away. I Need You. Ticket to Ride. Act Naturally. I've Just Seen a Face. He thought of Cara's face.

He turned out the lamp and pushed the boxes back as they were. Then he slid out, under the table on his stomach, back to his room. He crawled out the window with the record under his arm.

———

IT WAS A LONG WALK. HE STUCK HIS THUMB UP THE FEW TIMES HE heard cars approach, but none stopped. Not even when he walked along the side of 22, squinting in the summer sun, moving the record from one hand to the other, not really caring whether anybody stopped or not. He didn't get nervous until he walked around the long curve and saw the Super Stop and Shop. He wondered if there was like a night manager and a day manager or if just Jerry was the only one.

Tim walked into the parking lot and looked for the blue station wagon. He didn't see it. His heart beat faster as he walked across the lot to the front of the store. The automatic double doors opened and he walked through.

He pulled a shopping cart from the back of another and set the Beatles record in the front like a baby. He took a breath and pushed the cart through the second set of doors and into the store.

It was busy a little. Mothers pushed heavy carts full of food with their suntanned children in tow. Tim walked up and down the aisles, hoping to come across Cara stacking shelves. He watched the other shoppers out of the sides of his eyes. He saw a woman check the back of two different cartons of juice and he wondered what she could be looking for as he did the same. He placed one in the cart and pushed on, swallowing hard and looking away when someone looked over at him, picking something off the shelf and putting it in the cart. Like he was just totally shopping.

It felt good to be able to walk around the store with a cart full of whatever he wanted just like anybody. He thought that maybe Jerry wouldn't remember him if he saw him, and that he would look like everybody else. He pushed his hair over his eyes and put his head down, peering out as he moved down the freezer aisle in his hobo clothes.

Turning the corner, he hit Jerry from behind with the cart. Jerry said, oh excuse me as he turned, like Tim was a regular shopper. Then he glanced into the full cart—spaghetti sauce, cookies, juice, a pack of sliced cheese, mousetraps, hairspray, pickles, the Beatles record.

Tim pulled the cart back and started to turn it, saying, "Sorry sorry." Jerry walked quick in front of the cart and stopped him.

"What are you doing here?" Jerry asked.

"Me?" Tim asked.

"Of course you," Jerry said. "What are you doing in here?"

"I'm just totally shopping," Tim said.

Jerry looked into the cart. "No you're not," he said. "And you're not allowed in here. So you are going to leave right now or this time I will call the police. Do you understand? Do you think I won't?"

Tim nodded. He saw a woman look over. He felt his face burning. He didn't look like anybody.

"Okay," he said. Caught, defeated. He put the Beatles record under his arm and walked away from Jerry and the cart with his hands in his pockets and his head down. He walked past the lines at the cashiers but nobody really seemed to notice him.

CARA PULLED INTO A PARKING SPACE AND TURNED THE ENGINE OFF but left the car on to listen to the end of the song. She was early anyway. She pulled the key from the ignition and got out of the car, leaving the windows rolled down. She pulled the watch from her pocket so she could double check the time clock when she punched in. She walked to the front of the store, and when the automatic doors opened, Tim stepped out.

Cara's heart leapt and sank. "Hey!" she said, smiling, surprised. She looked past him. "You can't be here. If Jerry sees you here he is going to be super pissed."

"He just now kicked me out," Tim said. He shook his head as he looked at her and smiled and tried to not smile. "Hi."

"Hi," she smiled back. Then she looked confused. "Why did you come back here?"

"Why?" Tim asked. "What do you mean? I came to, like, because, to see you." He shrugged, sinking inside.

"I just really need this job right now," Cara said.

"Yeah," Tim said. "Okay. I'm sorry. I just wanted to like? This is for you."

Tim handed her the copy of Help!, blushing.

"Oh," Cara said. "Really?" She took the record and turned it over. "I love Ticket to Ride," she said. "Wow. That's so cool. It's like, when did you first ever hear the Beatles?"

"Yeah," Tim said and smiled. "You remember. Do you have that one already?"

"No," Cara said. "I don't have any Beatles records actually."

"Really?" Tim said. "Well? Now you do."

"Now I do," she said and looked him in the eyes. "Let me put this in my car. I don't want Jerry to see us, see it. Like with my stuff I mean, in the break room."

They walked through the parking lot side by side to Cara's car. She leaned in through the open window and slipped the record under the front seat, out of the sun.

"Was your dad really mad," Tim asked, "the other day when you were late?"

"Oh my god yeah. He was all like, it's about showing up. You need to learn how to show up and be reliable."

Tim listened. "Was your mom?"

"No," Cara said. "She never gets mad." She looked across the parking lot and shook her head as if remembering. "She was like, oh my god, all she ever does is show up! How much more reliable could she be? I was like, right?"

"That must be really nice to have her stick up for you," Tim said. "She sounds like a friend almost."

"Yeah," Cara said. "She is. She's like my best friend. I tell her everything."

Tim couldn't even imagine it.

Cara reached into her pocket and felt the watch. And in the silence Tim swallowed and said, "So, when maybe you have a night, a night off, when you don't work? Maybe we could like do like, I don't know, anything, something. Nothing. Together I mean."

Cara looked down, afraid to look at his face. "Yeah" she said, to say no, and he could hear it. "I don't really have nights off right now. I'm working a lot. It's probably not like a great idea right now."

Tim stood there looking down. He glanced up at her and felt the feeling he felt looking at her face sink into what he felt about everything else. "Oh," he said. "Really? I thought."

"Yeah," Cara said. "I know. I want to. I just shouldn't I don't think. It's not a good time. Right now." And she thought of her room, and the packed bags weighted and waiting, and for the first time she resented them. It scared her.

"Okay. Yeah. Sorry," Tim said.

"I just," Cara said. "It's not. Don't be. I am. It's hard to explain."

Tim told himself to give up and kept going. "Well," he said, hoping his voice might sound lighter. "Maybe after summer. If you're not as busy? Maybe just like on your lunch break, we could have lunch. Maybe with your mom even, I could meet her.

She sounds so cool. I mean, you met mine right?" He smiled small. Cara smiled back sad.

"That sounds really nice actually," she said. She rubbed the watch in her pocket. "But I gotta go. I gotta clock in."

Tim nodded. "Okay. Yeah me too. It's a long walk back to New Miltown."

Cara looked at him. "You walked from New Miltown to here?" she asked. Tim nodded.

"Why?"

Tim shook his head, confused at the question. "Why do you think?"

They looked at each other for a moment, not saying anything. Then Tim turned and walked away. Cara stood alone at her car. Halfway across the parking lot, he looked back and she was still there, watching him.

12

Tim walked back asking himself, what did you think? What did you think fuckin' idiot what did you think was gonna happen? And he was mad at himself for feeling so sad. Like yeah this is what you're sad about? He tried to push it back from his mind, and slow sang a fast song soft like a mantra as he walked. *I'm a customer a customer a customer.* He was in love with the girl who works at the store but he was just *a customer a customer a customer.*

Not true, he thought. No money. And the song made him wish since he was all the way out there that he could go to the little record store with the puppets on the walls where the bald guy with long hair sold incense and bootlegs and bongs. But he'd stolen from there a while ago, before he made himself change. He stole a Ramones t-shirt, the black one with the eagle. The guy had been so nice to him too, playing him records, giving him tapes, telling him about music.

He took the shirt because he wanted it, and because he was trying to be that way then. But he was terrible at it. Not the stealing part. He never got caught, except for the time he really did, but whenever he stole and especially when he stole that t-shirt, he felt poisoned afterwards. It made him feel like he was confessing to something, like he was telling the world that this is the only way he could get anything. He would only have it if he could steal it.

And he'd walk home red-faced and out of breath and he wouldn't even want to touch whatever he stole much less own it. And he'd stuff it under his bed or in the back of his closet where he couldn't see it. He did love that shirt though. He wore it every day those days like armor. But every time he put it on he thought of stealing it and he felt a chill inside that sometimes he called embarrassment and sometimes he called bad luck.

He didn't know where he'd get records anymore. And there was a new one he really wanted too. He had been waiting awhile. They didn't play it on the radio but he saw a drawing of it in a music magazine. It sounded great. It sounded like it might sound like how he felt. He didn't get to read the whole thing though because the guy behind the counter at the milk-and-shit was one of those Jerry Manager guys.

Tim had been at the magazine rack, at the back. The guy wouldn't have to see him even if he didn't lean way over the counter and look into the big fish eye mirror hanging in the corner of the ceiling like a moon. Tim flipped through the pages and looked in the mirror at the guy looking at him. One of those big lottery posters hung in the window behind him and every time he leaned over, Tim could see it read You Can't Win If You Don't Play.

Tim thought who cares if he's not bothering anybody reading a magazine no one's ever going to buy and he couldn't read it even anyway because the guy kept leaning over and staring at him. Tim was waiting for it, the guy shouted hey from behind the counter. He said, "This isn't a library."

"Oh it isn't?" Tim said. He put the magazine back in the rack and walked back down the aisle to the door.

"What are you a dummy," the guy said. "You a smart guy?"

"I'm not anything," Tim said. He pointed at him. "You're blocking the If You."

He thought maybe the library might get that record some day, maybe if he asked they would. But he wished he could go to that record store and hear it now. He bet that's where Cara got that shirt. Where else would she have. And he thought about Cara saying don't be, I am, it's hard to explain, and he just kept walking.

He figured he better go see Darcie. He'd been thinking about her since he'd seen her see him talking to Cara. He wanted to tell her he felt bad. But he didn't know if she'd be that sucks Darcie or you should Darcie.

When he had first told her about things, and she was the only one he'd ever told and her just hints, she would listen and say that sucks, oh my god, that sucks. And it made him feel like it was okay to breathe a little, even if some words fell out when he did. But then she started telling him you should. He knew she didn't mean it mean. He was a little younger than everybody maybe that's why. But then she went and told after she swore she wouldn't tell. And he guessed he'd never tell her anything again, much less everything, because she had promised. Still though, he thought. He should go see her.

He had been walking down the road for over an hour and still had another hour at least when he saw the pickup jabbed over onto the side of the road. He could see it from a far way off and when he got close enough he recognized it.

Tim walked up to it from the back. In the passenger door mirror he could see Dan's head knocked back, his mouth open. When he got to the rolled down window, he could hear him snoring. He held an empty beer can in his right hand, tilted on its side on the seat.

Tim stood at the open window. He thought this football

asshole. He thought thanks for nothing heavy metal. He said, "Hey." And again, "Hey!" Dan lifted his heavy head and looked at Tim confused. It was quiet enough so Tim could hear the wind through the leaves of the trees on the side of the country road, and the birds calling in morning.

Dan said, "You again."

Tim wanted to say why did you do that for the other day but he was scared to and what did it matter even now anyway. He said, "What are you doing?"

Dan sat forward. "I'm going to work. What are you doing, walking to England?" He shook his head. "What time is it?"

Tim didn't know.

Dan swore. He looked around at the empty cans in the cab and said, "I was just finishing this." He turned the key in the ignition. The engine sounded like a clock ticking. He turned it over again and swore. He tried a third time and swore again.

"Don't just keep turning it over," Tim said. "That won't do anything." Dan stomped the gas a few times and turned the key again. The engine clicked. "You're gonna flood it," Tim said.

Dan moved Tim back with the door as he opened it. He leaned to get out and fell onto the side of the road. He rolled onto his back.

"Woah you are fucked up," Tim said.

Dan sat slow. "You're fucked up," he said. "Your fuckin' hair's fucked up." He steadied himself on the side of the truck and stood. He looked like he was going to throw up.

"Well, but like are you okay I mean?" Tim said.

Dan looked over with naked clown eyes full of fear, like he was peering out from cracked greasepaint. "Of course I'm okay," he said. "I'm fuckin' wicked okay."

"Okay," Tim shrugged and looked away. "You don't look fuckin' wicked okay but."

Dan said, "Just." He motioned his hand to shoo Tim away.

He steadied himself on the side of the truck as he walked to the front and opened the hood. He peered inside.

He glanced over to see Tim watching him and reached for a random cap at the side of the engine compartment.

"Yeah," Tim said. "I don't think the wiper fluid is the problem."

Dan reached again.

"Woah stop," Tim said. "That's the radiator. That can burn you if you open it fast."

Tim leaned over and looked at the engine. He found the starter motor. "You got like a long screwdriver or something?"

Dan swayed as he walked to the back of the pickup bed. He looked at Tim and waved his arm over it like a spokesmodel. He stumbled back to the cab and sat behind the wheel with the door open. He shook the empty can on the seat and drank the last hot drops.

Tim walked back to the side of the truck and peered over at the tools and crumpled fast food takeout bags and empty beer cans in the back. He hopped up and leaned over the side, planking on his stomach to reach a long flathead screwdriver. "That'll work," he said.

Under the hood, he connected the contacts on the starter solenoid with the screwdriver. He called out to Dan. "Go ahead." Dan stared out at the green hills past the pastures, down the long stone walls, lost in lies he could tell his boss. Tim told him to go. Then to himself he said, "Story of my life all of a sudden."

Dan faced back to the steering wheel and turned the key. Under the hood the engine rumbled on with a shower of sparks around the screwdriver. Tim slammed the heavy hood shut. He stood outside the open driver side door as the truck idled.

Dan looked at him. "Did you seriously just fix that?"

"No I bet your starter is bad it sounds like," Tim said. "Not the starter itself I mean, but just like the solenoid."

"Yeah I don't speak, like," Dan said. "Outer Mongolian."

"Solenoid?" Tim asked. "It's just this thing that takes a little spark and turns it into a bigger one is all pretty much. It's pretty simple. When you turn the key, the electricity from the ignition goes into the solenoid and like closes these two big contacts that are in it, in the solenoid, and that starts the starter and the starter starts the engine. If the solenoid's bad, you gotta make the connection yourself. So that's why this."

Tim handed the screwdriver back to Dan. Dan shrugged.

"Anyway," Tim said. "Slide over." He was tired of walking.

"Why?" Dan asked.

"Cause I'm driving," Tim said.

Dan shook his head at the absurdity of it. "You're not driving my truck," he said.

"Man just move over," Tim said. "Don't worry I'll be real careful not to like ding it or anything."

Dan slid over and let Tim behind the wheel. Tim pulled onto the road.

"Well I guess we're even," Dan said.

13

Dan told Tim to turn right and pointed out the window. "That gray one," he said. Tim pulled up in front of the small aluminum sided house. There was a chain link fence with an open gate and an overgrown walk that led up to the porch. The storm door was off its hinges and leaning beside the doorway. "Here's good enough I guess," Dan said.

They got out of the truck. Tim handed Dan the keys. "Okay cool," Dan said. "I'm feeling way better."

Tim nodded, "Yeah okay, later." He turned back towards the way they came. They had passed the Carvel a couple minutes back.

"Where you gotta go," Dan asked.

"Wherever," Tim said.

"You want a beer?"

Tim shrugged. "Nah, I gotta, I oughta, like—"

"Sh'yeah you do," Dan said. "Come on. Why not right?"

Dan walked through the open fence gate and up to the porch. He walked with his arms out from his side and his chest out like he was about to get in a fight. Like he was about to beat up his house. He walked inside and left the door open. Tim watched from the side of the truck and then said, "Fuck it." He followed him in.

There was a wire spool table on the porch, covered in empty bottles. A black plastic ashtray choked with cigarette butts. Action figures of professional wrestlers lay scattered among the bottles. Tim walked inside, leaving the door open behind him.

Dan was in the kitchen with his back to Tim, dialing the phone. Above the little formica table was a shelf of cobweb-covered bric-a-brac. Little blue porcelain kittens and brown puppies and pink piglets were arranged around a cookie jar that looked like a panda, next to a bronze horse head and a stack of stars and stripes tea cups from the Bicentennial, with a bunch of Santa dolls and reindeer, and a mug that said Hang in There.

The wood paneled walls were plastered with posters and magazine photos of scowling heavy metal bands, skinny and shirtless and draped over each other, with dyed lion hairdos and pancake makeup and tattoos, and black leather pants and black leather vests and black leather tank tops and black leather underwear with silver spikes on them, pretending to laugh, pretending to scream, pretending to pout, thrusting pointed pink and snakeskin and polkadot guitars out from their crotches, giving thumbs up, giving the finger, pointing drum-sticks with their tongues out. There were posters of wrestlers too, hairless and swollen and slippery, with tight trunks and headbands and tassels, tearing off their tank tops, pointing big fingers and gritting their teeth with their eyes bugged wide.

Dan turned around and held his finger to his lips to tell Tim to be quiet. Then, into the phone he said, "Yeah hey it's Danny, lemme talk to Rick real quick?" He held the phone to his ear with this shoulder and paced the kitchen.

Dan pretended to throw a wrestling hold at Tim. "Man when I was thirteen I thought for sure I was gonna be a wrestler," he said. He flexed his bicep and pretended to kiss it, miming a pose from the wall. "I had the best name and everything."

He opened the fridge and took out a six pack of beer with one bottle left in it. He motioned for Tim to have it.

"Yeah what was it?" Tim asked.

Dan smiled. "Mr. Future. Like Mr. Wonderful, Mr. Perfect? Mr. Future."

"That is a pretty good name," Tim said.

"Right?"

Somebody spoke on the other end of the phone. Dan said, "Hey Rick man hey it's Danny. Man, I know what you are gonna say. And I'm totally, it's just my truck wouldn't start and—"

Dan listened and scowled. He reached over and opened the last beer as he cradled the receiver against his shoulder. Tim thought he was opening it for him, but Dan put the bottle to his open mouth and drank half the beer in one long swallow. Tim raised his hands but Dan didn't notice. He turned his head away from the phone and let out a long, silent burp.

"No," Dan said. "No I'm not drunk. It's not even like something o'clock in the morning. Of course I'm not." He listened for a second and then said, "No, no. See what it is, is like, I messed up my hand. It's kinda bad. So if I sound like." He listened for a second. "Doing you know, just nothing. I was trying to do a trick. No it is not Rick. No it is not fucking bullshit. No it is not. You should see my hand man. It's all smashed up so bad it's crazy."

Dan's eyebrows went up. "Oh nice, Rick. Real nice. Thanks a lot. *Before* I do? That's. I don't mean to be swearing but. That's very like. That's not cool." He listened, with his eyes narrowed, shaking his head. "Yeah? Oh yeah? Okay. And you know what? You know how you're gonna feel like when I do? Like an, like not good is all. But like really bad, I mean, when you see. Yeah? Okay. Fine. Yeah. Fine."

Dan hung up the phone. "Dick." He finished the beer and set it on the counter next to the empty pack.

"What's all that?" Tim asked.

"My boss. Doesn't believe I smashed up my hand. Says I'm drunk. Can you believe that?"

"Can I believe it?" Tim asked. "You are drunk. Your hand is fine."

"Still though!" Dan said. "Still. He doesn't know that. If someone's just got real hurt and just had an accident you shouldn't be all like that when they tell you." Dan shook his head. "That's not right. *And* I'm outta beer."

Dan opened a cabinet and took out the only bowl, with a spoon already in it and a box of cereal with a wrestler on the box. He filled the bowl, then opened the fridge and took out a milk carton. He tried to pour some over the cereal, but it was empty. He put the carton back in the fridge, then spooned a bite of cereal into his mouth. He looked over at Tim. "You want some?" he asked.

Tim shook his head. "Is this your house?" he asked.

"I guess so now. It was my grandma's." Dan sighed and took a bite of cereal. "She died."

Tim looked around. "She must have really liked Whitesnake. That who you get it from?"

Dan looked at Tim for a tense couple seconds. Then he shook his head. "Man she hated it. She'd always be like turn down that faggot crap I'm watching stories."

"Oh she'd say that?" Tim said. "That's not cool."

Dan took another bite of the dry cereal. He nodded. "She was nice but she was mean."

"Is this where you grew up?"

"Mostly," Dan said. "Yeah."

"With your grandmother?"

"Mostly yeah," Dan said.

"Where was your mom?" Tim asked.

"Fuckin' wherever," Dan said.

"Oh no way," Tim said. "That's where my mom was too. I wonder if they ever ran into each other."

"Yeah well if they did," Dan said. "I hope your mom was driving a truck."

———

TIM FOLLOWED DAN OUT OF THE HOUSE AND SHUT THE DOOR behind him. He asked Dan if he should lock it. Dan said, "What for?"

At the sidewalk outside the front gate, Dan said, "Hey will you show me how to do that with the solenoise?" Dan led Tim to the truck and reached into the driver window. He popped the hood and grabbed the long screwdriver.

"Solenoid," Tim said. "Yeah it's easy." He latched open the hood and pointed out the starter motor and the solenoid. "That right there is the starter, and that little thing right next to it is the solenoid. Just take the screwdriver and put the end of it there, right there on the positive terminal. And then you just drop it down and touch the other terminal with that end. Hold it there. I'll start it up. Watch for the sparks."

Tim sat behind the wheel with the door open. He said, "Are you ready?"

"No," Dan said. "Wait. Yeah. Go."

Tim turned the key in the ignition and the truck started with a burst of sparks around Dan's hand. He jumped back, smiling.

"It worked," Dan said.

"Yeah," Tim said. "You just gotta be careful where you make the connections."

"Right," Dan said. "Wait but what if you're alone though?"

"Oh," Tim said. "Then you're fucked."

Tim slid out of the pickup ready to leave. Dan lifted the hood up and clipped the hood prop into its latch. Holding the hood with his right hand, he gauged the weight of it. He placed his left hand onto the side of the engine compartment, looked at Tim and slammed the hood down on top of it. He lowed like a cow. He tried to lift the hood off his hand but he slammed it so hard it had shut. "Open it," he yelled. "Open it!"

Tim dove back into the truck cab and pulled the hood release. He ran to the front and lifted it enough for Dan to pull his hand free. It was already swelling. His fingers curled into a claw. Tim stood with his mouth open. "Oh my god," he said. "Oh my god why did you do that?"

Dan walked in a small circle, holding his hand in front of him. "Because fuck fuckin' Rick that's why! I'm not gonna let that guy tell me I'm lying and fire me."

"Oh my god," Tim said. "That is so fucked up."

"Yeah fucked up like a fox," Dan said. He turned his hand over and looked at both sides as it turned purple.

"It looks like a balloon animal," Tim said. "Did you break it?"

"No I don't think," Dan said. He held up his hand and tried to move his fingers. "It just looks bad." He winced.

Tim didn't know what to say. He really wanted to get out of there now.

"Hey, can you drive me somewhere?" Dan asked. "It's not far."

14

Cara was wearing the stupid red polo shirt with the logo on it and the stupid red visor with the logo on it, even though her hair was so short, even though she was back in the back over the grill where who could even see. The stifling air reeked of meat and fryer grease and sweat. She was four hours into the eight to four shift, the worst part of the worst shift of the worst job of all the jobs she'd had for two years of nothing but jobs. Fast food jobs. Dishwashing jobs. Grocery store jobs. Studying freezing in parking lots all winter and watching a second summer somersault past plate glass windows, while she stood inside on the insoles she slipped into her sneakers to make it hurt less to stand for hours chained to grills and cash registers and shelves. Three dollars an hour. Every minute a nickel, every penny a feather. Saving for wings.

The lunch rush lumbered up and in the back she slapped cold gray patties in tombstone rows over a flat black grill slick with gristle and fat. She stuck out her tongue in a fake gag. "So," she said, and shook her head in disbelief. "Gross."

Cara flipped several burgers at once with a long silver spatula and every time she had a moment to catch her breath, she was supposed to be cleaning. Around her, the others on the shift, some her age, some older, one lady really old, dropped fries into wire baskets or laid out buns in rows and squirted the buns with mustard from the yellow bottle and ketchup from the red bottle and put the seventeen wet dried diced onions on the bottom of the buns and the three pickles on the top of the buns. If they caught up with the orders really they should use that time to clean. Even that ten seconds, they said. Especially that ten seconds.

But Cara liked Gary, the manager. He rolled his eyes a lot and called her girl, stretching it out for emphasis. She flipped the last row of patties bubbling in fat and he peered around the corner with his eyebrows down, holding the phone by its long curled cord and covering the mouth piece.

"Cara hey," he said. "It's your dad. He say's it's an emergency, so, but it's picking up. You know how it is with the phone. And this is the shift where they'd check." Cara nodded and pursed her lips. Gary rolled his eyes at himself, and this whole place, and said, "Girl I'll get these," and swapped her the phone receiver for the spatula.

James had been vacuuming the house when Katy started crying for him. She couldn't find the little threadbare black stuffed kitty she called Lucky. At first he thought maybe she was pretending, and maybe she was, but the tears built until she wasn't. Until they got away from her and she was crying so hard she was coughing on the sobs. He didn't know what to do. He was supposed to help her, he thought. He was supposed to make it so she didn't cry like this, and she only cried like this with him, sobbing herself inside out. He didn't know what to do. He looked, he looked everywhere and told her she'll turn up, she'll turn up, sometimes things get lost. Sometimes we lose things. But that just made her cry harder. And she pushed her face into his chest and coughed tears. "Where did she go?" she said. "How could I lose her?"

He called Cara knowing he shouldn't. He stood in the kitchen and said embarrassed into the phone, "Hi could I speak to Cara please? Real quick sorry."

Exposed alone between the drive-through window and the deep fryers, Gary doing her job while the girls at the counter spun in fast circles between the registers and the soda machines behind them—setting trays on the counter while the soda carbonation deflated, hitting the button again to fill the cups, getting the fries getting the fries getting the fries, setting them on the trays, saying thank you, yelling "burgers" and doing it all again—Cara said, "Dad I'm not allowed calls. I can't talk."

"Katy can't find Lucky," James said.

"Dad you said it was an emergency!"

"She's screaming her head off," James said. Cara could hear Katy crying through the phone from far away. Somebody yelled we need burgers. Cara pressed the phone to her ear and put her finger in her other ear.

"Did you look?" she asked.

"Of course we looked," James said, shorter than he meant.

From the grill Gary asked, "Cara?"

Cara said, "Did you look under her bed, back by the wall?"

James said he hadn't. From the grill, Gary said, "Cara."

"Well that's where it's going to be," Cara said.

They called for burgers again. Gary said, "Cara. Seriously."

"Why?" James asked.

"That's where she puts it," Cara said. "It's there."

James asked why again. And Cara thought, really, why? She said, "Because." James started to say something again and Gary raised his voice, "Cara now. Seriously." And James repeated, "Because why?" and Cara yelled, "Why do you think?" She slammed the phone down. She went back to the grill and took the spatula from Gary.

Gary handed it over with his eyebrows raised. He knew how that was. He was taking care of his mom. Cara cleared the burgers from the grill and slid them into a stainless steel tray and pushed it under heat lamps at the end of the counter. She lined more patties on the grill. Gary nudged her shoulder with his shoulder. "They'll get their dang hamburgers."

At home, James listened to the dial tone and Katy crying. He placed the phone receiver back in the cradle. He went to Katy's room, where she lay in her bed, her face in her pillow, crying. He knelt down and slipped his head under the bed and reached all the way back. That's where Lucky was. Katy sat up and hugged him. She said, "Daddy you found her."

TIM PULLED DAN'S PICKUP DOWN THE DRIVEWAY OF THE JOB SITE and parked behind a couple other pickups. Inside the skeleton of a framed house, a few electrical and plumbing contractors installed the wiring and pipes.

Tim turned the ignition off. "I really can't stay," Tim said. "I have a lot of things, to like do or whatever. So."

"Two minutes, he'll be here. Just help me out, come on," Dan said. He held up his swollen purple hand.

"That looks like," Tim said. "Not good. At all. I don't think you should wait around."

"Oh he'll be here," Dan said. "Hey what are you, like a mechanic or something? Were you like Vo-Ag?"

"What? No."

"Where did you learn to do all that?"

"Just at the library."

"They have cars there?" Dan asked. Tim couldn't tell if he was joking. "You should do it," Dan said. "For like a job I mean."

"Why?" Tim asked.

"Uh," Dan said. "Because you know how to?"

"No like why would I want a job?" Tim asked.

"Uh," Dan said, drawing it out. "For money. Stupid. To be like employed."

"Yeah," Tim said. He glanced at Dan's hand. "Looks great."

A new red pickup about the size of a fire engine pulled in and drove up to the edge of the framed house. "That's him," Dan said. "Watch this."

"Watch what?" Tim said.

Dan got out of the truck and said, "Just come on."

Dan walked up to the red pickup. Tim followed but stayed behind. Rick lowered himself from the cab and hitched the belt of his khaki pants over his stomach. Dan called out to him.

Rick turned. "Oh here he is."

Dan held up his hand.

"Oh my god," Rick said.

"Yeah oh my god," Dan said. "Yeah. See? See? I told you it was crazy."

"Wait are you drunk too?"

"No!" Dan said. "Yes. A little. I drank after."

Rick shook his head.

"You wouldn't have a couple after if you did this?" Dan asked. "What am I supposed to do? This hurts. You said come here first."

"Go," Rick shouted. "Go get that fixed."

"See?" Dan said.

"Yeah, Dan," Rick said. "I see. See me seeing? You're not fired. Everything's roughed out, and these guys are wrapping it up and all this drywall is sitting here and I'm off schedule but you're not fired."

"Thanks Rick," Dan said. "Hey I was wondering."

"No," Rick said. "I told you last time no and it's no."

"Come on, man," Dan said. "What can I do? Look at this! I was counting on Friday. Can I just get for the past couple days and maybe spot me a day? Just so I can grab gas and groceries? I'll be fine next week. I'll get some Percs. I'll be fine."

Rick wedged his hand into his pocket and pulled out a thick wad of bills. He counted some and handed them to Dan. "I only can do eighty and I shouldn't even do any. And I ain't paying you for days you haven't worked ever. Ever. Period. The end. Never."

"Wow, thank you," Dan said. "That's perfect. Thanks so much man."

"Yeah yeah," Rick said. "This is it, Dan. You played great, but this is my business and you're throwing me off by like a week at least. I don't really care if you do quit fucking up or don't quit fucking up but you're gonna quit fucking up here for sure one way or the other."

Dan nodded and looked down like a child scolded. Rick looked over at Tim.

"What about him," Rick asked. "He wanna pick up your days?"

"Yeah maybe," Dan said. "Sure probably."

"He's kinda little," Rick said. He motioned Tim over. He turned back to Dan. "What's his name?" Dan tried to remember as Tim walked up.

"Me?" Tim asked.

"Yeah you," Rick said. "What's your name?"

"Tim!" Dan said.

Tim nodded, "Yeah."

"You ever hang drywall?" Rick asked.

Tim shrugged. "What's drywall?" he asked.

"It's how you put walls up," Rick said.

"Oh," Tim said. "Yeah, kinda."

"We can show you. It's not hard. You want his days?"

"How much?" Tim asked.

"Ten an hour off the books," Rick said.

"Yeah maybe," Tim said. "I guess."

"Oh you're welcome," Rick said. He stepped toward Tim. "Let me see your hands."

Tim looked up at him. "What?"

"Let me see your hands."

Tim held his hands out, palms down.

Rick snorted. "Other side, genius."

Rick grabbed Tim by the wrists and flipped his hands over. He rubbed his thumbs over Tim's palms. "Yeah right," Rick said. "No calluses. You never worked a day in your life."

"What?" Tim snapped. "Get your fucking hands off me. You fat fuck." He tried to pull his hand back and Rick held them tight. Dan stiffened.

"Watch it," Rick said. "Relax. All's I'm—"

"Fuck you relax," Tim said. "Get your fucking hands off me."

Rick clamped down on Tim's wrists hard and pulled him forward. He leaned down close into his face. Tim could smell his aftershave, the burger lunch on his breath.

"Are you a tough guy?" Rick asked. "You sure don't look like a tough guy."

"Are you a fuckin' dick?" Tim asked. "You sure do look like a fuckin' dick."

Tim stepped forward fast, hard enough to surprise Rick, and pushed him off balance. Just as quick, he pulled back and yanked his hands free. Rick stood there startled and mad. He glared at Dan and back at Tim.

"Get the fuck outta here," Rick yelled. He turned to Dan, "You too, Dan. I don't have time for this bullshit. Get out of here and take your little faggot friend with you."

Tim hocked to the front of his mouth with a loud scraping sound and spit in Rick's face.

Dan yelled, "Oh shit!"

Tim backed up as Rick roared and wiped his face. Rick lunged at Tim and grabbed him by the right arm. Tim turned his face to pull away and Rick punched him, full force, as hard as he could, to the right of his eye. Tim spun with the blow.

To him it was a flash of red and black and a dull thud, and then after that he saw Rick's red face and the big fist coming as if in slow motion, and then he saw the ground spinning fast as it turned him around. It was all out of order. First he felt the blow, then he saw it. He didn't go down though. And he hoped Dan saw all that and he thought, that's how you do it, as he ran down the driveway catching his balance.

"Yeah keep running," Rick yelled. Tim ran onto the road, with his hand over his eye. He could hear Rick calling behind him, "Keep running! Just keep running!"

15

Tim burned his fingers on the foil of the TV dinner and they each ate a piece of chicken but his was still cold inside. He gave Nicky the drumstick and the little square of apple pie. He moved the antennae until channel eight came in okay so they watched the show about the cruise ship where people fall in love and then the show about the place people go to make dreams come true. After that was the news, and he didn't want Nicky to watch it. Tim stood to turn it off and headlights streamed into the front window. He heard them yelling before the car doors slammed closed. He clicked the television off and said, "Quick come on."

Nicky scurried off the couch and followed Tim upstairs. They got in bed and turned the lights out and pretended to be asleep. Mick had been gone for however long and he had been back for a few weeks before everything started going wrong again.

They came in from school one day and he was at the table finishing a beer. Nicky dropped his book bag and jumped into his lap. He said, "Dad! You're back. You keep disappearing." Mick rested Nicky's head against his chest. He ran his fingers through Nicky's hair as Nicky listened to his heart. Mick said, "Ta da."

Tim didn't say anything. He brought his books upstairs. Mick never hit him but he charged the air around him with violence, and when Tim stole glances at the thick C of stitches scars train tracking his left eye he felt a cold stone in his stomach. He'd be gone and then he'd be back, gone then back. And when he came back there would be some money and there would be some groceries, even cookies. And Nicky who didn't remember would think that meant things were better, and that they would keep getting better. And then it always turned back to what it always was.

They came in that night screaming at each other, slamming the door behind them. Tim leaned over and turned the little radio on to the classic rock station and told Nicky don't listen to them. But the loud slurred words stumbled and crashed in the kitchen. They could only lay there and hear them.

"Did you?" Mick shouted. "Just tell me. Did you?"

"Get your hands off me," Nora screamed. "Get your *hands* off me."

Tim heard something break, dishes or glasses. And then he heard a dull thud loud against a wall and Nora yelled out in pain. Tim jumped up and stomped on the floor in his bare feet. He pounded on the door. He yelled stop. Stop, stop, stop as he banged with both fists on the door. Downstairs they were yelling at the same time, lost and caught in each other. He unlocked the door and grabbed the door knob.

Nicky leaped out of bed and threw his arms around Tim's legs. "Don't go down there," he pleaded. "Please don't leave." Tim let go of the door knob and paced the small dark room with his hands over his ears.

Nora locked herself in their bedroom and they argued through the door until Mick stormed out. He left the door open behind him. Everything was quiet. Tim laid on his back awake seeing every fight he had seen and hearing every fight he had heard. Nicky slept next to him.

It was Tim's idea. He had been thinking about it, over and over, twisting plans in his head until they knotted into something that seemed possible. That seemed simple as slipping out the window and going.

They had talked about it, pedaling their bikes slow down empty roads in their hats and coats. The first time, they rode out farther than they ever had before and Tim joked, "We should just keep going." Nicky's eyes lit up and he said, "Could we really do that? Like for real I mean?"

Tim turned on the little lamp he read by and slipped out from under Nicky's arm. He crawled quiet across the floor to the dresser they shared and pulled out Nicky's jeans with the knee patches, and a pair of his own jeans and a few pairs of socks. He emptied his book bag of his math and history books and packed the clothes. He found the pants and t-shirt he had worn that day piled at the foot of the bed and dressed, then pulled a sweater over his head. It had been cool for spring. He sat on the edge of the bed for what felt like a long time before he leaned down and nudged Nicky.

"Nicky," he whispered. "Nicky. I can't be here. I can't be here anymore." Nicky rolled over and looked at his brother. He said, "Me neither then." Tim nodded, so desperate the plan in his head made sense.

Nicky sat up worried. He said, "I left my sneakers in the kitchen." Tim said he would get them. He said, "Stay here. Don't follow me." And he slipped as quiet as he could out the bedroom door.

He looked in the dark kitchen but Nicky's sneakers weren't there. They were next to the front door, kicked off next to the abandoned book bag when they came in from school that day.

They didn't have to go back for two whole weeks. Nobody would even know they were gone.

Tim picked up Nicky's sneakers but put them back down and turned to the closet door. He stared at it for a minute and then carried a chair from the kitchen. He opened the closet slow so it wouldn't creak and stood tiptoe on the chair to reach the shoe box on the top shelf. He knocked the top off the box and reached in. He felt the barrel of the black Charter Arms .38 revolver. He picked it up by the handle with his thumb and index finger pinching the grip panels and lifted it from the box. It was lighter than he thought it would be.

Tim rested the gun on the floor by Nicky's sneakers and then slipped back into the kitchen with the chair. He closed the closet door and picked up the small revolver, holding it in his fist by the short handle, pointing it at the floor, careful not to touch the trigger. He stepped soft up the stairs with the revolver in his right hand and Nicky's sneakers in his left.

When he slipped through the cracked bedroom door, Nicky was sitting dressed on the edge of the bed. He handed Nicky his sneakers, and then held the gun in his palm to show him.

"You found it," Nicky said.

"I knew where it was," Tim said.

"Can I hold it?" Nicky asked.

"No," Tim said. "Come on, let's go."

Nicky double knotted his sneakers as Tim slipped the revolver into the bag under the clothes. He grabbed three comic books to read to Nicky and the book he had been reading about the boy his age who runs away and lives alone in the mountains. They could do it. He knew they could.

"Maybe we better shouldn't go," Nicky said. "I don't think."

Tim said, "Nicky you don't have to but I can't be here. I can't be here anymore." Nicky looked at the floor.

They both knew Nicky wouldn't stay without him. He

couldn't. So he said okay and took a deep breath that stuttered with the threat of tears. Tim bunched up a sweater and slipped it over Nicky's head, and put his red cap on him and looked at him and said, "Are you sure? Are you ready?"

Nicky nodded but he looked worried. "Where are we going to run away to though," he said.

"I don't know yet," Tim said. "Maybe we'll just keep running."

Tim slid out the bedroom window and reached back for his book bag. Nicky climbed out after him and followed Tim to the edge. Tim placed his hands to his side and slid off the roof, spinning to lower himself down. To Nicky it looked like Tim had been swallowed whole by the darkness below.

"Tim," Nicky called in a loud whisper. "Tim!"

Tim hushed him sharp from just below him. "I'm right here. Just lay on your stomach and slide down. I'll hold your legs."

Nicky started to cry. "I can't," he said. "I can't see you."

Tim shushed him again. He said, "You're gonna wake them. I'm right here."

"I'm scared," Nicky said. "I can't see you."

"Don't be," Tim said. "I'm here. I'm right here. Come on."

Nicky bit his lower lip and slid back on his stomach and dangled his legs off the roof. He felt like if he let go he would plummet into nothing, if he fell he would fall forever. But then Tim grabbed his legs and lifted and lowered him at the same time. When he was on the ground, Tim said, "See, it's not even that far down."

Tim fixed Nicky's sweater and straightened his hat. He picked up the book bag and said let's go. They walked down the alley together alone, passing through the yellow halos of the streetlights into darkness.

16

W hen they got to the edge of the sidewalk, Nicky stopped and looked at the dark road ahead of them. "Why can't we ride bikes?" he asked again.

Tim turned back. He had explained twice already. They wouldn't get anywhere on bikes, two little kids riding bikes down 22 in the middle of the night. "They'd catch us in like two seconds," Tim said. "We have to get off the road."

He had told Nicky to crouch down when cars passed, but none had. Just the empty Bonanza bus headed south. They watched it go by, the lonesome driver and the black empty windows. It would be morning in a few hours, though, and there would be cars on the road then. Everybody would see them.

They stepped off the end of the sidewalk and walked along the side of the road, their sneakers soaked through from tall wet grass. The Buddy's parking lot was empty and the neon beer signs in the window were off.

"We can cut through here," Tim said. He started across the parking lot and Nicky ran to catch up. He pulled Tim by the sleeve.

"No," Nicky said. "I don't want to go back there. Look how dark it is there."

"Nicky," Tim said. "We can't stay out here. Do you want to get caught?"

"I don't want to go anymore I don't think," Nicky said. "I changed my mind I think okay? Can't we go home?"

"It's just dark now," Tim said. "It's not gonna be dark forever."

He reached over and took Nicky's hand and led him across the parking lot to the side of the bar. They crept sideways to the back. Nicky thought he heard something and he froze with fear, squeezing Tim's hand hard enough to hurt.

"Will you stop?" Tim whispered. He pulled his hand back. "There's nothing there."

"Can I carry it?" Nicky asked.

"No," Tim said.

"Will you?"

"No. We don't need it. Just come on."

Tim pulled his hand free and led Nicky to the back of the building. Nicky stopped in the shadows outside the security lights of the back door. "I have to pee so bad," he said.

"Oh it's okay," Tim said. "You can."

"Where?" Nicky asked.

Tim pointed to the dumpster and the stacked cases of empty bottles beside it. "Just go back there."

"No," Nicky said. "No. It's too dark."

"Oh my god, Nicky," Tim said. "I'm right here. Just go."

"Come with me," he said.

"I'll be right here," Tim said.

"Please," Nicky said. "Just stand with me?"

Tim sighed and they walked over to the dumpster. Nicky looked around and then stepped between the dumpster and the cases and unzipped his jeans. He looked around again.

"Where's Dad's gun?" he asked over his shoulder.

Tim shushed him and said, "It's in the bag, Nicky,"

"Will you hold it just in case?" Nicky asked. "While I go?"

"No," Tim said. "We don't need it. There's nothing here. Just pee already."

Nicky turned back and stared down at himself. He shifted from foot to foot. Then—he couldn't help it, he didn't want to, he wanted to be as sure as Tim who always seemed so sure, he wanted to be brave, he tried not to—he started to cry. "I can't go," he said. "I have to go so bad but I can't go."

He sounded terrified. Tim hated it when Nicky cried. He was so quiet. He'd sniff hard through his nose hoping no one would notice but it made his whole body shake. Tim didn't know what to do. He couldn't go back.

He stepped closer to Nicky and talked soft into his ear. "Breathe slower," he said. "Breathe through your nose, slow."

"I can't go," Nicky said.

"Yes you can," Tim said. "You have to."

Nicky tried to take slow breaths through his nose as his heart raced and the tears pooled in his eyes. His thin shoulders raised and fell. A single sharp sob slipped from him. He just wanted to pee. Why couldn't he what was wrong with him why did he always cry like this why was it so hard to breathe just like in school just like reading out loud just like when it was almost lunch and he got scared the bigger kids would be there and he would want to see Tim why did he always get like this?

"I'm trying I promise," he said. He sniffed, the tears choking off the words. He took a breath. "Tim I'm trying so hard I promise. I have to go but I can't go I promise I'm trying."

Tim wished he could carry him when he got like this. Wished he could put him in his pocket and carry him until he felt better. He leaned forward and whispered in Nicky's ear.

"Just take the slowest breath," Tim said. "Everything is going to be better, I swear. So much better. Just me and you. We can do it. I'm right here."

Nicky nodded but he wasn't sure. He looked down at himself and took a breath. He looked over his shoulder at Tim.

"Will you sing it?" he asked.

"Oh, Nicky, no," Tim said. "Please no. Come on. You're okay. You can do it."

Tears welled in Nicky's eyes. "Please?"

Tim shook his head. "Okay okay."

Tim looked down at his feet and cleared his throat. He tried to remember how the song started and thought back to their bedroom, to Nicky stopping everything whenever it came on the radio.

"What's the first—"

"You should have seen," Nicky said.

Tim shook his head and ran through the first few lines, whispering them fast to himself.

"Yeah, that's right," Nicky said, his voice a little brighter. He looked down at himself and waited for Tim.

"You should have seen by the look in my eyes, baby," Tim started. He sang soft and halting, about how there was something missing and about how he tried to talk about it but they didn't listen. "Come on, Nicky."

"Keep singing," Nicky said. "It's working."

"I forget and I forget," Tim sang, humming over the lyrics he couldn't remember. And then the chorus came to him and he sang to Nicky, his voice cracking on the high parts, about how he meant everything he said and that he meant that he loved him and would love him forever and that all he wanted to do was keep on loving him. He sang the chorus again and he could hear the trickle of Nicky peeing into the gravel.

"I'm done," Nicky said.

"Good," Tim said.

Nicky zipped his pants and turned. He looked at Tim impressed. "You sing that really good," he said. "You sound just like him."

"Oh great," Tim said.

And then Nicky hugged him so tight and it felt so good. It felt so good to be away from there and be together, and it was spring and it would get warmer and he knew everything would be okay.

"All right all right," Tim said. He hugged Nicky back and lifted him off the ground. He set him down and turned toward the tree line, leaving his arm around his shoulder. "Let's go."

THEY WALKED HUSHED THROUGH THE THICK OLD GROWTH FOREST in the blue gray light before sunrise, below the towering canopy of maple, birch and beech, red oak and white ash and hickory, their tall gray trunks tear streaked with lichens. Still chilled from night, they moved silent and small, stepping across the pits and mounds of tree throws, climbing over the moss mottled boulders of the low rolling mountainside.

In the primeval quiet Tim felt like they were being drawn deeper into the forest as if on a still and beautiful sea like in his dreams. But he'd get tangled and tethered by memories back to the dark trap of the house, and it would seem like they had never even left at all.

"They always yell," Nicky said, reading Tim's memories out loud to him. "Why do they have to fight like that?"

"Because they're drunk all the time," Tim said. "They're always drunk."

"Oh," Nicky said. "Yeah." They walked a few paces in silence.

"I'm never gonna get drunk," Nicky said.

Tim said, "Yeah," and kept walking.

Nicky didn't like the way he said it. He frowned. "You either right?" he said.

"Of course me either," Tim said. "Why would I want to even? Look at it."

"Uh-huh," Nicky said. "But promise."

Tim looked over at Nicky. "I just said."

"I know," Nicky said. He stopped walking and leaned against an old cypress tree. "But do you promise? Do you like promise promise I mean."

"Yeah," Tim said. "I *promise* promise."

Nicky nodded. "Can we stop yet? For a while? My legs hurt."

Tim nodded. "Yeah," he said. "Let's rest for a while."

Tim walked over to the foot of the cypress and set the bag down. He sat and pulled his knees to his chest. Nicky dropped beside him. He rested his head against Tim's shoulder and yawned. "What time is it?" he asked.

"Almost morning maybe," Tim said.

Nicky fell asleep against him. Tim rested his head back against the tree and closed his eyes. They had done it. He listened to the soft rustling of the forest around him and slept.

THEY DIDN'T SLEEP LONG. TIM WOKE TO THE SOUND OF THRASHING and Nicky shaking him. He didn't know where he was for a moment. He thought he heard someone scream you you you. He jerked his head around and pressed back into the trunk of the cypress. The sky was lighter, almost sunrise and everything was quiet except for their breath, panting in fear.

"What was that?" Tim said. They heard branches breaking in the dark cluster of trees in front of them. There was something like a scream, a you or a no, Tim couldn't tell. It was a person or an animal. It seemed so close.

"It's there!" Nicky shouted and pointed, and Tim thought he saw branches moving. "It's big, it's big!"

The panic inside Tim's chest felt like a string of firecrackers. Where had he brought them? What had he done? At the next scream, Tim grabbed the book bag and started pulling out the clothes until he had the revolver in his hand. He didn't know what to do. He'd never shot a gun before. Never even pointed one. He fumbled it in his trembling hand, his thumb slipping on the hammer. Nicky was crying and pulling the sleeve of Tim's sweater, yelling, "There, there!"

In a moment of quiet, Tim caught his breath and thought maybe it was over. It was nothing. Maybe a deer but it was gone. But deer don't make noise. The next scream was much louder, seemed much closer now, and the thrashing moved the long branches of a hemlock tree just in front of them.

"It's coydogs," Nicky cried. "It's bigger it's bigger." He pressed his face into his knees and covered it with his arms as the trees thrashed and the terrible cry seemed to come right at them.

Tim pointed the gun shaking in both hands towards the sound. He'll scare it. He'll scare them away, he thought, and aimed at the trees and then looked away and then looked back.

Nicky screamed, "It's coming." And as Tim realized he didn't know if there were even bullets in the revolver, he hadn't even thought to check, wouldn't have even known how to, his shaking hand pulled the dual-action trigger with a sharp thunder of gunshot, then another, then another, the recoil causing him to fire again and again, the trigger cocking and releasing five times, louder than anything he had ever heard and then clicking clicking clicking against the chambers.

The silence sounded empty as death. Blue still nothingness. And the sweat rolled down his neck cold as a finger and he realized he needed to breathe now so he did as best he could. In the sickening minute that followed the shots, Tim couldn't unclench his fingers from the gun's grip and he had to shake his hand to jerk it loose. He dropped it to the forest floor and looked down at his hand. His trigger finger was bleeding.

Half sitting, half standing, he dug his heels into the pine needles and pressed himself against the trunk. With Nicky curled with his head in his hands on the ground next to him, Tim pushed himself up, scraping his back against the rough bark of the cypress. It was so quiet he thought he was deaf. All was still. It was like nothing had happened.

Tim stared at the thick trees in front of them, the dark blue sky lighter now, the waning crescent moon wincing low behind them. When he looked over, Nicky was standing next to him. They walked forward together in slow scared step. When they reached the dense cluster of trees and Tim saw, his heart fell from his chest. "Oh no," he said. "Oh no no no."

A few yards in front of them, the little brown dairy calf looked up at the boys with stunned wet eyes. It took shallow breaths and did not thrash or cry or move at all. It's thin front legs were splayed in front of it. One back leg was tucked under its body and the other twisted back at an awful angle, its hoof wedged between the trunks of two young intertwined ash trees. It had gotten caught trying to climb through them.

Of the five shots, Tim could see he had hit the calf twice, once across the top of its neck and once in its side, where dark blood trickled from a small clean bullet hole. Nicky stepped up and nudged the belly of the calf with the toe of his sneaker. The calf did not move. It lay there breathing soft and blinking slow as it stared at them. Tim pulled Nicky back.

"Don't," Tim said. "Don't do that." He looked down at what he had done and sobbed. "Oh god," he said. "It's just a baby. Oh god. Look at its foot."

Tim hung his head and cried what felt like years of tears. He said, over and over, "It's not fair. It's not fair."

He turned to Nicky, standing next to him with his hands in his pockets, looking at the calf with a blank, accepting expression. "He must have got lost," Tim said. "He must have wandered off and got lost. Look at his foot. He was all caught up. He was just trying to get loose."

Tim watched the calf take its last soft breaths and lay still as a shadow at his feet, dead. They stood over it quiet, Nicky waiting for Tim to say something or move. When he didn't, Nicky broke the silence.

"At least that's what they're only born for anyway," Nicky said, trying to comfort him. "That's the only reason they have them, is to kill them when they get big enough."

Tim shook his head no.

"I mean so don't cry," Nicky said. "Because it was going to happen anyway."

Tim hung his head as he walked forward past the calf. Within twenty yards he walked through the tree line into an old pasture that had been neglected and was falling back into forest. Past a collapsed stone wall, he could make out a farm. Past that, he could see the road, and the back of the sign for Buddy's outlined against the sunrise.

They had been walking in circles in the dark. He turned back and met Nicky walking towards him. Nicky turned with him, and they walked back past the body of the calf.

Tim found the gun and picked it up disgusted, hating it, hating everything about it and where it had come from and what he had done with it and who it had made him. He shoved it into his back pack and stuffed the pairs of jeans and scattered comic books on top of it.

The sun rose as they followed the tree line towards the sound of traffic, the doppler gusts picking up as they got closer. They emerged from the woods together and stood like blades of grass by the side of the road. They walked home heads bowed, exhausted and not talking, and many cars passed them, but nobody stopped. No one even seemed to see them at all.

It was a clear blue cloudless morning when they got home. Tim threw the book bag onto the sloped edge of the roof and pulled himself up. He lay on his stomach and reached down for Nicky. Tim let Nicky go through the open bedroom window and then sat for a moment unsure if he had the strength to pull himself through. He was so tired. Nicky poked his head through the window and looked at him sitting there, and then Tim turned and made it in.

Tim sat on the edge of his bed and kicked off his sneakers. He was about to collapse down onto his thin pillow when he remembered the gun and the gut punch of fear woke him. Nicky laid down and Tim sat up. He crawled over to the bag and pulled the gun from it. Nicky watched in silence. Nicky thought Tim looked like he was glowing the way glow in the dark glows, but the soft eerie green was sadness. Tim stood. The revolver seemed to buckle him forward like it weighed a hundred pounds.

Tim slipped sideways down the stairs and moved quiet down the hall. He opened the closet door as slow as he could and then sat the gun on the floor. He got the chair from the kitchen, and when he stood to reach the top shelf, he felt the lid for the box, still off. He put the gun back and slid the lid onto the box. When he had left it off, he imagined them finding it, when they were long gone, and knowing they were serious. But nobody even knew they had left.

In her bedroom, Nora laid on her back. She had been awake all night watching her life. She listened to Tim's soft footsteps. And she thought of her two sons, hungry and feral and incredible, the one dark and smart and sensitive and observant, and the little her, blonde and tough and burning with worry. What would become of them, she wondered, alone and frightened. What would become of them if this was her now?

Many hours later, she checked on them and they were still sleeping. Curled together like for warmth, barefoot in blue jeans and sweaters. Nicky was splayed out on his back, one arm hanging from the edge of the bed as if reaching. Tim slept on his side next to him, his arm across Nicky's chest as if to protect him and keep him close, even in sleep.

THEY SLEPT ALL DAY AND DEEP INTO THE EARLY MORNING. NICKY woke up in the middle of the night and stared at Tim sleeping next to him until he could see him in the dark. It looked like he was having a nightmare. Nicky rolled on his side, with his back to Tim, and pulled Tim's arm over him. He pressed his back into Tim's chest and held his forearm close to his heart, holding him back and hoping that in the dream Tim would know he was not alone. He fell asleep.

Tim slept through the night and did think he was dreaming when he woke for a moment and the room was red with sun. Nicky wasn't there and Nora sat on the edge of his bed. She was feeling his forehead for fever. He said, "I'm not sick I am just so tired." Then he fell back asleep.

He woke alone. The room was bright and a warm breeze came through the open window. He walked down the stairs and the living room blinds were open and the room was full of light. Nicky was on the couch watching a space adventure cartoon. The table was clear and the room was clean. How long had he slept? Everything looked so different.

Nicky turned and smiled at him. "It's G-Force," he said.

Tim said, "Oh." He walked into the kitchen. The blinds were open in there too, and the counters had been cleaned off and wiped down. Tim squinted. He was awake.

Nora stood at the sink with her back to Tim. She unscrewed the top off a half empty gallon of vodka and poured it into the sink. She turned and dropped it into the trash and it clanged against another bottle. She saw him standing in the doorway in his jeans and t-shirt. He looked so thin.

Tim stared back at her. She smiled. She pushed a strand of hair behind her ear. There were bruises on her wrist and forearm. Nicky appeared in the doorway next to him.

"There's my boys," Nora said. "There they are."

"What are you doing?" Tim asked.

"I'm cleaning up," she said.

"Where's dad?" Nicky asked.

Nora sighed. "Nicholas, honey," she said. "He's gonna be gone now."

Nora looked at Tim and Tim looked back. He nodded. She stood in the kitchen like a seedling leaning to the sun, so yellow in the light. She looked different.

"Are you hungry?" she asked.

"Yeah we are," Nicky said.

"I can make breakfast?" Nora said.

"Really?" Tim asked. "What time is it?"

"It's late," she said. "But you want me to? Does that sound okay?"

"That sounds really nice," Tim said. His soft voice cracked. "That sounds really good mom." Nicky looked up at him.

Nora turned and opened an empty cabinet, and then another. "How about?" she said, and opened another cabinet. She pushed aside a few cans and some boxes. She said, "I could make." She shrugged and turned back. "Maybe spaghetti?"

Nicky said, "Spaghetti for breakfast?" And Tim shot him a quick sharp look to quiet him.

"Yes please," Tim said.

"Does that sound okay?" Nora asked, relieved.

"That sounds really good," Tim said.

"Yeah?" she asked.

"Really good," Tim said.

She turned back to the shelf. "With maybe." She opened the refrigerator. "Is just butter okay? There's really not much here."

"There is," Tim said. "There's enough."

17

Tim walked down the street toward the Carvel with his bell rung, punch drunk and a little dizzy. His eye was swollen and sore but he could still see out of it. Everything hurt and he didn't know where to go, so he went to Darcie.

Darcie had just finished her shift. She changed out of her Carvel clothes in the bathroom with Round and Round stuck in her head again. She smiled goodbye to the girl behind the counter. As she reached the door, Tim pulled it open, frowning like an hourglass, the dark bruise stretching from eye to ear like half a mask.

Darcie held the door open and stopped him with her hand soft on his chest. "Woah," she said. "What happened to you?"

Tim said hey but his throat felt tight. His eyes were dry but she could tell he had been crying. Darcie pushed him back and stepped out of the Carvel with him. She took his wrist and led him to the picnic table near the dumpster. Tim sat on the table top. Darcie stood in front of him and lifted his chin to see his eye.

"I told you you should look where you're going," she joked. He kept his head down.

"Did your mom do that?" she asked, soft. Tim shook his head.

"Tim," she said.

"She didn't," he said. "She really didn't. This dick did it. Some boss guy. I was trying to get a job."

"You were trying to get a *job*?" Darcie said. "*You* were trying to get a job?"

Tim nodded then shook his head.

"Wait," Darcie said. "You tried to get a job and the guy punched you in the face?"

Tim shrugged. Darcie laughed.

"It's not funny, Darcie," Tim said.

Darcie nodded. She touched his face to see his eye again. "Just sit there," she said. She went back inside and came out holding a Flying Saucer ice cream sandwich wrapped in cellophane.

"I'm not hungry," he said.

"It's for your eye dummy," she said. She sat next to him on the table and held the Flying Saucer against the bruise. He reached up to take it, holding his hand on top of hers for a moment. He brought his hand down to his knees, and Darcie lifted it back up and put the Flying Saucer back on his eye.

"Keep that there," she said. "That guy dotted your I for sure. I should have grabbed a whole Cookie Puss."

Tim shook his head. "I hate it here," he said.

"Yeah?" she asked. "Right here? Sitting on a picnic table, in summer, getting Carvel, with me?"

"No," he said.

"Oh but that's all that's happening," she said. "Here."

"Oh god Darcie come on," he said. "Please with this Donahue shit. I'm like begging you."

"It's not anything," she said. "I don't know, Tim. It's like I always tell you. That like sometimes it's when things hurt really

bad is like the only time when we can see things really clear.
Like how they are."

"When do you always tell me that?" he said.

"Like every time we ever talk," she said. "It's like you're in this
little box and there's this little hole you look out of and you
think that what you see is everything there is."

Tim closed his eyes. "Okay," he sighed. "Whatever."

"That's better," she said. She moved closer to him and he
leaned against her. They watched the cars pass. "It's like that
song you used to always play," she said. "Hey ho, let go."

He studied her. "Let's go," he said.

She smiled at him. "I thought you'd never ask."

Darcie slid off the top of the table and turned back to him.
She placed her hand over his and brought the Flying Saucer
down. She leaned over and kissed his bruised eye, letting her
lips rest soft as breeze for the slow sweet sad seconds.

"Ouch," he said.

"You got that right," Darcie said. "See you around maybe."

———

AFTER THE SUDDEN NOTHING THERE WAS DARCIE. WHEN IT WAS
the endless empty in a hole as big as Nicky. When the wound
was gaping and he couldn't breathe and he couldn't scream and
he couldn't sleep and he couldn't eat and he moved confused
through the halls small and lost as a moth. When the black hole
sucked the last sliver of sunlight from his life and the glue fumes
blew behind his eyes like a blowtorch. When it was fuck them
that's why when it was no why at all when every answer was I
don't know or nothing, there was Darcie. When he was dazed
and nocturnal and forgotten, when he was peering in windows
watching church people watching incomprehensible football,
when he lived at the back of the town library reading joyless

anything to silence his mind until they blinked the lights, when he started stealing, when he mixed all their liquor cabinets into one most empty bottle and drank it like strychnine on the roof, hoping he would die, when he pulled down his sleeves and hid his wrists, there was Darcie.

There was acidwash aquanet Bon Jovi Darcie with her crocodile smile and her beaded diamond doublewave knottedheart fishtail chevron friendship wrists and her cup of coffee eyes behind her drugstore readers and her ballpoint VH peace sign jeans and her pink calculator. There was that sucks oh my god that sucks Darcie with her willow soft skin and her chemical flower hair and her Cinderella pin and her Ratt pin and her Crüe pin and her endless arms that reached and wrapped around him as he Dream On shivered with his bare skin sticking to her car seats sweating in winter. With her first kiss braces scraping against his front teeth and the tip of her whisper secret tongue parting his bitten blistered lips and her slow hands that had done it before but not like this not with anybody she liked like this. When there was nobody forever, all of a sudden there was Darcie, flickering in the nightfall like a firefly like a tiny reminder that someday summer could come. When he was cut up and busted and in-school suspended she came out of nowhere. She sat there. She moved the desk closer. She saved his life.

She only knew a little though. Just the shreds and threads he told her in vague evasive answers and even that felt like too much. She had once heard a teacher say his name in a concerned whisper. She knew who he was but she had only ever said one thing to him. On the first day in homeroom, when they were calling attendance.

He sat right in front of her. When the teacher got to his name, he squeaked "here." And they all laughed. A boy behind her Mickey Moused it back, *"here,"* and they all laughed again. Tim turned, red eared and sinking smaller, and looked right at her. He saw her not laughing. When he turned back, she leaned forward and whispered from his shoulder, "Kids suck."

She saw him in homeroom that year but he never talked and he walked in the halls alone close to the lockers and didn't look up much. His clothes didn't fit. Some were too big and some were too small. He always looked like he was somewhere else. But when they announced the honor roll in the morning at the end of the first semester she heard his name crackle over the speaker and she thought woah, that kid? But nobody else seemed to notice him. He kept to himself. And she never saw him in the cafeteria. And she never had a class with him. Just homeroom. Just him then her. E then G.

She didn't know it was him when Mr. Abbot asked her to stay a minute so he could ask her a favor. Maybe she could help him with something? A boy was struggling. But she didn't know who when she said sure Mr. Abbot, she just felt happy to be asked. She went home and told her mom and dad.

She showed up outside 204 that day after the buses had left and the halls were empty. Mr. Abbot was waiting for her. He waved her over when she came down the hall. She said, "Am I late?"

In detention, Tim heard her but he didn't know who it was. And he sat there and looked at the clock and looked at the cardboard taped over the window and he said, to himself, *"One two three four five six seven eight,"* and he growled the guitar riff that followed and the descending chords and tapped the beat with his thumbs on the desktop. *"Now I wanna sniff some glue,"* he whispered. And he rubbed his fingertips together and made a little dirty ball out of the rubber cement that covered them. His head hurt.

Mr. Abbot met Darcie down the hall so they could talk. "Hi

Darcie," he said. "No no you are not late at all. I just wanted to make sure he was in there."

Darcie nodded, not understanding.

"Do you know Tim Essup?" Mr. Abbot asked. She understood then.

"Oh it's him?" she asked. "Oh wow. Yeah. No I don't. I mean, I know who he is for sure. But I don't think he knows me. We were in homeroom last, freshman year. He was nice. Quiet. I sat by him. E and G."

"Oh sure, of course," Mr. Abbot said. "It's my first year with him. He might be a bright kid. He started great, but then. He's having a tough year. I'm not sure if you heard, he—

"No I know," Darcie said. "I heard about it for sure."

"So yeah," Mr. Abbot said. "He's having trouble participating. Understandably of course, but he has fallen pretty far behind. And he won't respond to me when I try so I thought maybe he'd let you help, just to get him up to speed. You're not as scary as a teacher, and I can tell you both sure like music."

Darcie smiled and looked down.

"Who knows?" Mr. Abbot asked. "You know? But maybe just take him through the stuff from the past few weeks or so if you can. You know it as good as anybody. See if he can follow along. If he catches on any, great. No pressure though. I just figure it's worth a try. Couldn't hurt, right?"

Darcie said, "Sure, Mr. Abbot."

Mr. Abbot took a breath and opened the door without knocking. He stepped into the room and stood at the blackboard, with Darcie nervous and looking at the floor next to him. She hadn't seen him in a while. He was taller than last year but he was just bones. He looked like the science room skeleton with his hollow eyes and his frozen stare.

"Knock knock," Mr. Abbot said. "Hey Tim." He waited a second for Tim to answer and then he said, "Hey Tim do you know Darcie Giuseppe? Maybe from homeroom last year? E and G?"

"Hi Tim," Darcie said. He glanced at her. He remembered. He shook his head no.

"Well so," Mr. Abbot said. "Anyway. Darcie is in my other class and she's about my very best student. So because it isn't really clicking with me," he held his hands up in front of him, "News flash. Stop the presses. Right? Just kidding. But I thought maybe you might want to work with her instead to catch up. So I asked her and she was nice enough to say sure. Does that sound like something you'd like to do?"

Darcie smiled and pretended to rub her nose. She looked down and then looked up with her lips closed. Tim looked at her and said, "No?"

"Okay," Mr. Abbot said. "Up to you. But you know, you're here anyway for the detentions. So maybe Darcie, would you mind just hanging out for a little bit? Do you need to go anywhere?"

"Uh," she said. "Yeah. No I mean. I don't. I mean okay?"

"Great," Mr. Abbot said. And then he left and Darcie thought, woah wait, he's leaving? And then she was standing there at the blackboard like she was a teacher and he sat there at the desk looking at her like what.

Darcie moved to a desk near him. He didn't look at her. She cleared her throat like she was telling a joke. He glanced over at her and then looked back away.

Darcie slid the desk a little closer and the metal legs squeaked against the tile floor. Tim didn't look up. She did it again, pressing down on the desktop to make the screech louder.

He still didn't look at her, so she did it again, this time even louder. He looked over. She blinked at him, pretending she hadn't moved. He looked away and frowned. She pulled the desk closer in a long loud scrape against the floor. And when he didn't even look, she moved the desk close in a fast series of short loud scrapes until their desks were almost touching.

Tim rolled his eyes. "Okay okay," he said. "I think that's pretty close." He put his hands under the desk and pulled down the frayed sleeves of his white thermal. She smelled like orange peels and rose petals.

She nodded at his t-shirt. "Ramones?" she asked. "Are they good?"

Tim shook his head. "Yeah." He put his arms on the desk, his fingers just out of his sleeve. He made little balls with the rubber cement.

"So," Darcie said. "I hear you suck at math pretty bad."

Tim glanced over. "If you say so."

"What's that all on your fingers," she asked.

Tim looked at his fingers. "Airplane glue."

Darcie nodded. "That'll do it."

She pulled out her binder and opened her math folder. She found last Friday's quiz and said, "Did you guys take this one yet? Was there a hard part do you think? What did you get?"

He looked over at her quiz with the red hundred circled and circled again. "I got a zero," he said. "I guess you only get smiley faces in them if there's two."

She wondered if he was making fun of her. He didn't sound like he was making fun of her. "Oh then. Well," she said. "Sometimes when you're doing really bad that's just like the best place to start doing better."

Tim rolled his eyes. Darcie flipped her book back a chapter and read through the section introduction out loud. Tim closed his eyes as she read and then he stared at the clock as the second hand sank to the six and then climbed up again. But then he looked at her, with her big hair and her grandmother bifocals and her eyebrows all up at the fascinating math. He watched her lips shine as she read.

She finished and then she looked up and thought oh he's looking at me and said, "So like," and explained what it all meant. She asked, "Does that make sense?" He shrugged but it did. She looked over and said, "Cool. Should we try to solve some problems?"

She drew an axis on a piece of graph paper. "So yeah, so Cartesian coordinates. Like, yeah they have big names and stuff and so they sound hard but all's it is is how you can tell where something is. And if you have two sets, you can figure out what the relationship between them is. Like, here look, say x equals two okay?"

She looked over at Tim as she marked the spot on the paper. "X is across, that's how I remember. Across, a cross? Get it? And y equals one, right? For this one. And on this one, up here, x equals five and y equals two. Those are the Cartesian coordinates for those two points, that's how you find them."

He watched her as she talked, her hand close by her mouth.

"Hey," he said. She almost jumped.

"Am I going too fast?" she asked.

"No," he said. "Why do you keep covering your mouth like that? Is it cause of your braces?"

Darcie covered her mouth. She thought so what, what does that have to do with anything? She felt her face get warm. "Whatever," she said. "They're ugly I know. They suck."

"Oh no I don't mean like that," he said. He shouldn't have said anything he guessed. "Sorry. Just."

"Oh is there food in them, gross," she said. She rubbed her tongue across her teeth with her lips closed.

"No," Tim said. "It's just. Is it cause they're broken?"

Darcie thought what? Oh my god, what? She looked down at the text book and wished she could crawl into it and close the cover behind her. She thought who is this kid?

"They're just the part on your teeth," he said. "The like." He didn't know the right word.

Darcie looked at him. "The brackets."

"Yeah," Tim said. "There's no like, you don't have the wire, the wire that goes across. There isn't the like."

"The arch wire," she said. "No. I know. Most people don't notice." Why did he, she wondered. What was he even looking at? Why would he say even? "That's what connects them. It broke. It's just. It costs a lot, even just for that. Okay? Can we keep going? Maybe this should be the last thing we look at. Let's just try to do one at least."

Tim nodded. "Okay."

Darcie looked up at the clock and then reread the problem. She forgot where she was.

"When did it break?" Tim asked. "The arch wire I mean."

Darcie stopped reading. She looked up at him. She waited. "Last year," she said.

"Oh," Tim said. "They've been like that for a year?"

"Yup," she said. "So okay? Can we keep going? Do you want to try to answer this one? Do you think you could find the relationship between these two points?"

Tim looked at her. She was so embarrassed. How could anybody be embarrassed in front of him, he thought. He shook his head.

"Not really," he said.

"Okay," she said. "That's okay. Sorry."

"Because like." He reached over and took the pencil from her, touching her hand for a moment. He placed the point of the pencil to zero. He looked over at her and thought, whatever. "Because like this is a two-dimensional medium?"

"Because what?" she asked.

"I mean you can find some things fine with Cartesian coordinates on an x-y plane, but it's better I think to understand them like in space," he said.

Darcie shook her head. "What? Did you say in space?"

"You're trying to represent a three-dimensional concept with a two-dimensional model," he said. "That's just paper. It's not like the world. It's funny kinda that they call it Cartesian because you can't look at it from all angles like that. Get it? But so if you want to really find the relationship between two points, you should have Cartesian coordinates in space."

He drew a third line through the point where x and y met. "Imagine that's coming off the page." He drew an arrow at the top of the line and wrote the letter z above it.

"Wait," Darcie said. "What?"

"So now like," he said. "Each point can be represented by ordered triplets instead of just two coordinates. And then you can start to figure out like the functions, and then you can find the rate of change and the limits. And a lot of times, stuff like that, like tangents and velocity and rate of change? That's all the same problem. But remember, the rate of change isn't always constant. That's a common mistake. That people, like. Make."

"Wait," Darcie said. "What? What is all that?"

"I don't know," he said. "I suck at math pretty bad."

"But really what is that though?"

"It's just like," he shrugged. "Calculus."

"It's calculus?" she said.

"It's the study of limits," he said. Then he shook his head. "But that's just the super basicest stuff. Just the beginning stuff. I don't know it that good. It's just interesting."

"But how do you know that?" she asked.

"I just read about it," he said. "We got to how you'd only need two points to understand the relationship between things and that didn't sound right so I looked it up."

"But so why are you faking then?" she said.

"What?" he bristled. "I'm not faking. I'm failing math. I'm failing everything."

"But you know all this then," Darcie said. "If you can look up calculus and understand it you can know geometry. You have to actually. Why are you flunking?"

"I know what I know," he said. "Why do I have to tell them what I know? Why should I care if they know what I know or not?"

"But that doesn't make any sense, though," she said.

"Because fuck them then that's why," Tim said. "Does that make sense?"

"No," Darcie said. "Not really." She leaned forward and spoke in a soft voice. "Because like that's not how it works though. That's like the actual opposite of how it works actually. You know?"

He shrugged.

"You're pretty stupid for a genius," she said.

Tim smiled a little, for the first time in a long time. Darcie closed her binder and the text book and put them back in her book bag. Tim handed her the pencil. He extended his arm out of the sleeve of the dirty thermal under the Ramones t-shirt and she saw all the cuts. He'd gotten most of them from pulling his fist out of the plate glass, not punching it in.

"Woah what happened?" she asked.

Tim pulled his hand back and pulled the sleeve down and put his arm under the desk.

"It's okay," she said and thought that was a weird thing to say. She zipped her bag. When she looked back at him, he was just staring at the desk again. "Well," she said, not knowing what to say. "Okay."

She stood and picked up her bag and walked to the door. She looked back at him.

"They gave me more detention for it," he said.

Darcie nodded. "Oh," she said.

"No I mean, but so like," he said, and he sat up and leaned towards her. "Maybe you could keep teaching me then?"

Darcie laughed. She laughed, to him, the best laugh ever.

"Yeah," she said. She put her hands in her pockets and rocked on her heels a little. She smiled. "Yeah I guess I could help you out."

Tim smiled back a little. "Cool," he said. "But just like, for real? Don't tell okay?"

She looked at him and nodded, serious. "I won't."

"Promise?" he asked her.

"I do," she said.

18

Cara stepped on the pedal that moved the groceries towards her on the checkout conveyor belt. The young mother in front of her pulled cans of beans and a bag of rice from the cart, as her daughter leaned and reached for the candy bars. She pulled her daughter's hand away, and then pulled her last few groceries onto the cart. Not thinking, Cara rang up the candy bar the little girl had snuck between boxes of spaghetti.

"No," the mother said. "Not that."

"Oh sorry, sorry," Cara said and voided it. She smiled at the mother who looked back tired and checked the register to see the price with the minus sign. She handed Cara two five dollar cash shaped food coupons, with a large, cracked Liberty Bell arced with stars on the left, and on the right the words, this is an equal opportunity program.

Cara put the food stamps under the drawer with the others. While the mother counted out coins for the last couple dollars, and the people behind her in line frowned, Cara slipped the candy bar into her bag. She took the change from the woman and smiled at her. She told her, thanks, have a good day, and the mother just nodded tired and pushed the cart with her daughter and the few groceries towards the door. Cara wondered how old she was, like twenty-two? Not much older anyway than she was now. Maybe even older than her mother was when she'd had her, Cara thought.

Cara looked at the watch she set next to the register. It was all almost over but her heart felt heavy. Her legs hurt from standing and she thought of Tim walking all that way to see her and how he looked like he was getting smaller when he turned back to see if she was still there and how hard it had been not to run across the parking lot after him.

The next shopper had loaded all his groceries onto the counter and was waiting for Cara to pull them forward. "Hey," he said. "Are you working or not?" She nodded and rang him up.

When she clocked out, her check was in the slot with her timecard. She carried it with her to her car, and opened the envelope when she sat behind the wheel. She stared at it but it didn't look different or special. Sixty three hours, minus taxes, $168.84.

It was the last sixty three hours of the two thousand three-thirty-five-an-hour hours it had taken her to save for the whole first year tuition and money for books and money for housing and money for food. It was the last day of the last week of at least twenty-five hours a week for the past eighty weeks.

Alone in the parking lot in the blue station wagon, she stared down at her name on the paycheck. "Mom?" she said. She wiped away a tear. "Mom, I did it."

———

KATY WAS SIX AND SHE LAID NEXT TO CARA ON HER BED, WITH HER head on Cara's shoulder as Cara read to her. When they got to the part with the lion, Katy pulled Cara's long black hair over her eyes.

Katy said, "That lion is scary."

"It is," Cara said. "That's why the donkey wishes he was a rock." Cara lifted her hair out of Katy's face. "Give me my hair back," she said. Katy laughed. Then they heard the crashing sound from the bedroom, and James yelled in a thick slur, "Give those back the keys Kathleen." Cara pointed to the illustration and kept reading.

Kathleen closed the bedroom door so the girls wouldn't hear, wouldn't hear as loud at least she guessed, and turned back to James. He swayed in the middle of the room with his arms out like a tightrope walker, blind drunk and losing balance. She touched the thin silk scarf she had wrapped around her head to cover the last downy patches of hair she had left. She leaned on her cane, the car keys in her left hand.

James held his head in his hand and then looked up at Kathleen, with a dazed confused look, like a hurt boy. He reached for the keys and tried to balance. Kathleen gripped the cane.

"You wanna see me do my Jim Rice?" she said in her thick Dorchester accent. "You stay right where you are, James. You're drunk and you're not taking me anywhere."

James fell as he sat back onto the edge of the bed and slid to the floor. He stayed paralyzed with shame as the room spun around him. He held his head. Kathleen watched him. "Sleep it off James," she said. "We're gonna need you after."

Kathleen walked into the kitchen and gathered her purse and the car keys, but she felt weak and winded and she leaned against the counter. She called out for Cara.

Cara appeared in the doorway. Kathleen caught her breath. "Grab your little shadow," she said. "Time for that driving lesson."

KATY SAT BEHIND CARA AS SHE DROVE WITH KATHLEEN QUIET
next to her looking out the passenger window. Cara clutched the
wheel too tight, angry and sad, nervous to be driving. "I hate
him so much," she said.

Kathleen looked over and frowned. "Hey with that," she said.
"You watch it there. And watch the road too for crying out loud.
Don't get me killed on the way to chemo. Defeats the whole
purpose."

Kathleen looked at the leaves turning red and gold in the tall
trees alongside the river. "I always loved November," she said.
She sat quiet for a minute and tried to think of what to say. She
tried not to think too much, of what her words should be. But
more and more she understood that all the words she said now
would be among her last words, the words this daughter, dark
and smart and sensitive and stubborn, would remember and
carry with her forever. It made the words harder to find.

"Your father is a good man, Cara," she said. "He's just sick."

Cara looked over at her mother, with the scarf where her
long red hair used to be, and her green eyes shining in the
caverns of her cheekbones, her skin thin and white as birch
bark.

"Oh he's sick?" Cara asked. "*He's* sick."

"Yes he is," Kathleen said. "Absolutely he is. He's sicker
than me."

Cara's eyes filled with angry tears. "No," she said. "No."

Kathleen shook her head. "Cara, baby," she said. "I understand. I do. But you don't know what you think you know."

"How don't I know?" Cara asked. "Don't I see him right
there? On the floor? Don't I hear him yelling in the middle of the
night?"

"You do," Kathleen said. "And I know that's what you think

you know. But you can never tell looking at somebody. Did you know by the time your father was eleven he had gone to fourteen different grade schools? Did you ever hear that? Your grandfather, who you never had the pleasure to meet thank you Jesus, was a piece of work. A real piece of work. Mean drunk. Maybe the meanest. Your father used to lay in bed and listen to him beat his mother with a broomstick. A broomstick. He kept it in the closet. Your dad got the belt. And his little brother and sister just got a hairbrush or the back of a hand. That's why your father started being such a troublemaker all the time. He did it to catch the beatings. When his father would go after your Aunt Ellen or your Uncle Johnny, your dad would provoke him worse and take the punishment so he'd leave 'em alone. Said he tried to tire him out. Eight years old. Trying to tire him out."

Cara wiped a tear from her eye.

"Yeah, see?" Kathleen asked. "You didn't know about that. Anyway, so one night, he's laying in bed and his father starts going after your Grandma Dorothy in the kitchen. She was screaming. He must have been about twelve then. If that. And he said he didn't know what to do but he had to do something. So he goes running down the stairs, and he comes into the kitchen and his father's standing there with his back to him, holding that broomstick. And he yells, You leave my mother alone goddamnit! Loud he said. And his father turns, with this funny look on his face, and there's a butcher knife sticking right out of his father's chest. About six inches in. Blood everywhere. Grandma Dorothy had had about enough of that garbage. Didn't kill him though if you can believe it. Missed his heart by about a quarter of an inch."

Kathleen turned and looked at Katy, listening quiet and still in the backseat. She reached over and squeezed her knee. "Almost there," she said.

She turned back to Cara. "That sure got the state involved

though," she said. "Social workers. Foster care for a while then back again. And that's about when your dad started sneaking into the whiskey. He'd wake up with nightmares and he'd slip downstairs and take a nip. And it helped. What can I tell you? It's complicated. Cara, it helped him and it wrecked him. Helped with the nightmares, helped with his confidence. He'd sneak just a little bit to help make it easier. And it has been on his back ever since. For his whole life, since he was just a little boy. He didn't stand a chance with it. He never had a chance. It got him from the first sip. And he beats it, and then it gets him again. Every time he gets real scared, or his life hurts real bad, it gets him. And it's as bad now as I have ever seen it. Because, look at me. He's scared to death. But that man has loved me with his heart wide open since we were seventeen years old and he has never once put a hand on me. Or either of you. And he loves you like you hung the moon, young lady. Like you hung the moon. And he has from the second you were born. And he doesn't know how to say it, or what to do. He doesn't think there is anything he can do. He's survived things we can't even imagine and he still doesn't ever think he's strong enough for what's coming. But he is. I know he is. He is just full of fear and it's got him again. It's got him. So yeah, honey. He's not bad, he's sick. So you just watch it with your quick opinions, there, about my husband. If you please. Cause you don't know the half of it. Not the half. And you two are gonna need each other. More than either of you even know."

Kathleen caught her breath and watched the river. She turned back to Cara crying as she drove.

"Okay," Cara said. And the tears in her eyes got heavier.

"Alright, alright," Kathleen said. "Enough of that. There will be plenty of time for that later."

"It's not fair," Cara said.

"Fair," Kathleen said. "Ha. Fair's where you go when you

wanna see the chickens win the ribbons. You get what you get, kiddo. You get what you get. But there's always something to be grateful for. A lot. If you're brave enough to look. Don't forget."

Kathleen looked through her purse and pulled out a five dollar bill. She nudged it into Cara's pocket. "Drop me off for this crap and then take Ms. Pac Man back there for a Carvel or something," she said.

"By myself?" Cara asked. "I don't have my license."

"Yeah," Kathleen said. "Don't get pulled over."

Kathleen pulled down the visor and straightened the scarf in the little mirror. "This thing," she said. "I look like a pirate."

Cara laughed through her tears.

"Yeah laugh it up," Kathleen said. She reached out and stroked Cara's long dark hair. "My little black Irish beauty."

19

Cara didn't know how to have nothing to do. As she sat in her car, she remembered the Carvel girl's wristfuls of bracelets and thought she should get some embroidery floss so she could make them with Katy. A special one for each of them for when they missed each other.

She looked out her window and thought of Tim again, walking head bowed across the parking lot away from her. And from deep in her heart she felt what she wanted more than what she didn't want for the first time in such a long time. She reached into the glove box and found a pen and an old blue supermarket flyer that said Limited Time Offer. She walked over to the payphone and called information.

"In New Miltown?" she asked. "Is there an Essup?" The operator said there's a Michael and Nora and gave Cara the number. "Wait," Cara said. "Do you maybe have the address too?" She wrote both on the flyer, then fished a dime out of her pocket and dialed.

The ringing knocked Nora out of a gray Kadian nod. Slumped on the couch, she sat up and watched the phone ring until it stopped.

Cara slid her finger off the payphone hookswitch and placed the handset back into the cradle. No answer. The dime dropped into the coin slot and she put it back in her pocket. She looked at the address she had written next to the number and walked back across the parking lot to the station wagon.

TIM WALKED AWAY FROM THE CARVEL WITH HIS BLACK EYE ACHING and his fingers sticky with ice cream and bits of cookie. He felt lost and thirsty and alone, and he thought about how Darcie got the song wrong. The words she said felt like they were flickering in him, and he thought of holding his finger to Nicky's lips and telling him to make a wish, and the slow soft breath on his fingertip, and the hush of the waterfall.

He passed the empty bench of the bus stop and walked to the end of the sidewalk. He stood there and looked at the double yellow lines of the road stretching past Buddy's to nowhere and thought he better go home.

NORA STOOD AND STRETCHED AS IF WAKING FROM SOME DEEP REAL sleep and shuffled through her endless ruins. She slipped under the table and crawled through the tunnels of all the paperbacks she had read to Mick after he had done two years and could never read again without thinking of what they did to him in there. "A year for each ounce," he told her when they met, just weeks after his release. "I'm glad they didn't give me the ten. We never would have met." He had just turned nineteen. It was his first offense. He never read again.

Instead she read to him, grabbing paperbacks for a nickel at the library book sales. "Get anything," he had said. "I like everything. Your voice the most." Even after he stole their first TV from that motel before it opened so she could watch while she nursed the baby, he said he'd rather listen to her read.

Under the table she looked at the creased and broken spines, all the worn dogeared memories of some kind of love buried under the sprawling heaps of loneliness. She pushed through and sat by the pretty deco lamp and opened her box of old photos. Tim as a baby. Tim as a toddler holding newborn Nicky. Mick holding both the boys, one in each arm, leaning on the Triumph seat beaming next to her. She remembered that day— figuring out how to set the camera timer and racing over just in time to be next to him. "I hope it turns out good," Mick had said. It was the only photo of them all together as a family.

Too high to cry, she stared at the pictures and then turned to her lost friends. She opened a box of records and remembered when they shaped the air around her like weather. Oh this one, she thought, and pulled out Pearl. She got it when it came out, right after she'd met Mick, and she played it over and over, admiring the cover. "Now that's the way to be," she once told him. "She looks free." A few days later, she got pregnant.

Nora slipped the record back into the box and pushed it away. She opened other boxes, all the boys' drawings, all Tim's report card As, all the little scraps she gathered when Nicky hid them. She was the same way. She saved everything. She stayed back there for as long as she could. But the sadness rose as she came down so she crawled out and went back to the couch.

She was high again when Tim got home. He was headed around the back to go in through the window but he noticed the front door was cracked open. He thought he better check. He never knew.

He slipped in silent and saw her, floating with her back to him, slow and swaying like she was dancing. "I'd like to do a song of great social and political import!" she declared. "It goes like this."

She sang the hippie prayer in her poisoned honeyed voice, lost in herself and so far gone. She closed her eyes and raised her hand, and she asked God for a Mercedes Benz, and she asked God for a color TV, and she asked God for a night on the town.

When she finished, she turned and saw him, standing there with the shit kicked out of him, thin and pale as a candle flame, watching her. "That's it," she whispered.

She approached him slow and reached out to touch him but he stepped back. She leaned forward to look at his face, a hundred miles away. He stepped back again.

"What did they do to you?" she asked, wondering if he was really there.

"It's nothing," he said. "It's over."

"What is?" she asked.

He stared at her and thought of ways to explain but it was too late. What did it matter now. "Everything," he said. And he walked up the stairs, so tired from walking, and he shut the door behind him, ready to mean it.

20

I
t was a Friday. He had been at the library that night. He'd finished his homework for the whole weekend and was just bored, killing time, reading music magazines and looking at the pictures in a book about history. When they flicked the lights on and off, he put the book back on the shelf and walked out.

He shouldn't have taken the ride, he told himself a million times. Nora had been doing better for a while then. She'd seen a doctor who asked her if she had ever heard the word psychopharmacology. She took a new medicine. She cleaned the pretty houses set far back from the roads between the lakes. Sometimes she sat and had coffee with the ladies she worked for after she finished, talking about books or the president. The people she cleaned up after liked her, thought she was well read and eccentric.

She would work early and then be there to pick up Nicky because Tim had gone into ninth grade by then, taking the long bus ride along the river to the regional high school three towns over. Nicky would beam when he'd see her. And when he would stutter for breath telling her about a hard day or how they had laughed when it was his turn to read or how the teacher frowned when she looked in his desk, she would put her hand on his shoulder and pull him closer and tell him, "Honey whatever. It's not a race." She would hold his hand as they walked. She would make it better. They had that connection and Nicky was younger. He didn't remember the things Tim remembered. For Nicky, all that had passed and he worried when Tim stayed mad about things that happened back when everything was different. Nicky felt like it made Tim stay there and he didn't want to be there anymore. He liked it here, now.

But Tim couldn't help it. And he missed Nicky. He felt left out. Even when Nora would call him over to sit by her on the couch to watch TV with them, he would feel this force push him away. "It's like a magnet but backwards," he told Nicky, but Nicky didn't understand. They still shared the bed, but when Tim thrashed from the nightmares, Nicky would slip downstairs and crawl into bed with Nora instead. And when Tim would wake and find himself alone, he resented Nicky for leaving him.

It was the calf. He kept having a nightmare where he was alone in the woods and it was looking at him as it died, and it was trying to tell him something he needed to know in order to find his way home, but when it opened its mouth, blood came out. He didn't tell anyone. Who could he tell? It would scare Nicky. Maybe it would make him have the nightmare too even. The gun was gone as his father but some nights when he woke from the nightmare he could swear he was holding it and he would sit up in bed shaking his clenched hand to drop it like he had that blue morning in the woods.

He hated school. He wished he'd never skipped grades. He missed seeing Nicky's eyes peering into the diamondwired glass windows of the classroom door because he'd lost his lunch ticket and didn't know what to do. This school made him feel very far away. And the other kids were huge and stupid and mean. Sometimes they pushed him from behind and he'd think of the fight between Mick and Bennetts and wish he could be like that, but the memory made his chest tighten and his legs tremble.

A couple kids were nice, he guessed. There was this older kid, this kid named Shane. One day after school, they were the only ones in the school library. He swore and Tim looked over. He held up a copy of Of Mice and Men. "You ever read this?" he asked. Tim had. Shane waved him over and said, "Is this right?" Tim walked over to his table and Shane pointed to the top of the first page. In big block letters, somebody had written George Kills Lennie. Tim shook his head and said, "Well not till the end. It's good anyway though." Shane laughed and threw it in the trash in a way Tim thought was tough and cool. He offered Tim a ride home so he wouldn't have to stay for the late bus, and Tim had him drop him a few blocks away instead.

WHEN HE LEFT THE LIBRARY THAT NIGHT IT WAS GETTING DARK. HE walked a ways and then Shane pulled up beside him in the passenger seat of a car with three other kids in it. He said, "Hey Tim, what are you doing?" Tim told him nothing and he said, well come hang out then. Tim got in the back seat next to some stocky kid whose name he never even knew.

They drove around for a while and Tim listened to the older boys talk about girls from school in ways he thought were dirty and mean. He looked out the window and liked Shane less and less but tried to push the feelings away because he didn't really have any friends. Shane and the kid driving were whispering to each other in the front seat. Shane turned around and looked at Tim. He said, "You wanna get wasted?" The other two kids in the back said hell yeah and Tim made himself smile and nod and hoped they didn't see him when he looked away and swallowed hard.

The kid driving pulled down a street and drove slow, with the headlights out, and stopped outside the church. Tim got out of the car with them but he didn't understand.

"What are we doing?" Tim asked.

"Shut the fuck up," the big kid who had been sitting next to him hissed. Shane gave the kid a look. He waved Tim over and whispered, "Don't worry, it's easy. We do this all the time."

They walked around the side of the church to the parsonage. Shane tried the handle of the back door. "Holy shit," he said. "He locked it."

He turned to Tim and said, "This is where the pastor lives." Tim looked past Shane to the dark windows of the house. He thought he saw a light. "He's not here now," Shane said.

The kid driving pointed down and said, "Check it out." Tim looked. It was the dog door. Shane laughed and turned to Tim. "Can you can fit through there?" he said. "Don't worry, there's no dog anymore."

"I guess," Tim said. "Why though?"

"Just go through there," Shane said. "That's the back mudroom, then there's the kitchen, and like right outside the kitchen is where he keeps the booze. He doesn't lock it. Grab a couple bottles. It'll take like two seconds."

He didn't want to do it but he did it and it only took a minute. He slipped through on his belly and crawled across the floor to the kitchen. The light over the oven was on and the kitchen was clean. It smelled good, like somebody had cooked a nice dinner. He walked slow into the small clean living room, lit by one lamp on a desk with a bible. Tim grabbed two of the fullest bottles and carried them back through the mudroom. When he crawled out they all ran back to the car. Inside, he handed them over the front seat to Shane. The kid driving looked over. "That's fucking vermouth," he said. Tim didn't know what that meant. They all groaned. The kid next to him said, "Who is this little nerd?" Shane held up the bottle of Bushmills. "We're good," he said. "This one hasn't even been opened."

They drove down some dead end road and turned up music Tim pretended to like and passed the bottle around. Every time one of the kids sipped, the others would yell, go go, to get him to drink more. When it got to Tim, he took a long pull right off, his first ever drop, and they said woah and yeah, but it felt like pouring flames down his throat. And the bottle went around, and went around again, and then again. It didn't make him feel cool or confident. It just scared him. And then everything started to spin and blur. He missed the door handle three times before he yanked it open and fell out, throwing up on the ground and on himself. He felt the wet grass on his cheek and t-shirt. He heard the laughs. He didn't know where he was.

The next thing he remembered Shane was holding him hard under his arm and dragging him up to the porch and through the front door. His legs were like rope under him. He didn't remember telling them where he really lived.

Shane was almost drunk as Tim, and they stumbled on the stairs as they climbed to the bedroom. Nicky woke pinned to the bed with fear. Nora had kissed him on the forehead after he'd gotten into bed and told him she'd just be gone for a minute. He asked are you going to find Tim and she said no, don't worry. I'm just meeting a friend for a second. That was a long time ago he thought and now he was alone and too scared to even reach and turn the light on.

The bedroom door flew open and Tim stood there looking like on TV when the dead people come back, and there was some big kid towering behind him, holding him up. He let him go and Tim collapsed to the floor. The older kid said, "He's all fucked up," and left.

Nicky jumped over to Tim and tried to roll him over. Tim said, "I'm all fucked up. I'm all fucked up." And he smelled like he was sick. He reached out for Nicky but he missed. He tried to raise himself up on all fours but fell back flat to his stomach.

Nicky said, "Oh Tim. You promised." And he wedged himself under him as he tried to get up again and pushed with all his strength to get Tim into the bed. Tim was saying words that didn't sound like words at all and Nicky kneeled by the edge of the bed like he was praying and looked at him. He untied Tim's muddy sneakers and pulled them off. "Oh Tim," he said. "You promise promised. Now look."

Tim had passed out. Nicky crawled into bed next to him and laid close, his shoulder blades pressed to Tim's chest, like he did when Tim had the nightmare. He reached back to pull Tim's arm around him, but it fell away as if lifeless. Nicky pulled his t-shirt up over his mouth to soften the gasoline of Tim's breathing. He laid there as if alone and somehow, much later, he fell asleep.

———

NICKY WOKE TIM WITH HARD SHAKES UNTIL HE PEERED OUT FROM under the dull ugly pain of the hangover with one eye open. He saw Nicky sitting blurry next to him on the bed as angry as anybody had ever been at him. Each shove from his little brother felt like a bat swung to his head and sour waves of nausea bubbled from a swamp in his body and stung hot at the bottom of his throat. He tried to breathe slow and soft through his nose, to let it pass but Nicky kept pulling on him. Everything hurt.

"Oh my god Nicky stop," Tim whispered. He pulled the pillow over his head and saw flashes of the night before. Their sneering faces trading insults, the wet grass on his cheek as the ground tilted, wiping vomit onto his forearm. He didn't remember getting home.

"You said," Nicky started and Tim moaned to quiet him. "You said you'd—"

"Stop Nicky," he said. "When did I come in?"

"You didn't come in," Nicky snapped. "Some big kid, some kid I don't even know carried you in. Right into the room and everything."

"Okay okay," Tim said. "Just let me sleep again. I can't get up yet."

"You promised, Tim," Nicky said. "You promised."

"Stop," Tim said.

"And things are even okay now, things are even okay and mom's even better even," Nicky said, his voice constricting and his breath getting shorter. "And you promised and now everything is gonna, you're gonna make it like it was and you're—"

From under the pillow, Tim begged, "Stop."

"You're gonna make everything bad again," Nicky said, and pushed him hard to get him to sit up and be him again.

"Oh my god," Tim said, his head splitting. "Just stop, Nicky. No I'm not. It's one time."

"One time? So what one time!" Nicky yelled, furious. "How many times do you have to break something to make it broken?"

"Stop, Nicky."

"One time," Nicky said. "That's how many times. One time."

Tim pulled the pillow off his head and swung it hard at Nicky, knocking him back off the bed. "Leave me alone," Tim said. He put the pillow back over his head to block the light and pushed down the wave of nausea that swelled from his movement.

Nicky scrambled over to the window and yanked it open. Tim looked out from under the pillow. "Good," he yelled. "Go!"

Nicky scurried out the window to the edge of the roof and

lowered himself down. His breath was fast and ragged. He raced to where their bikes leaned against the back of the house and grabbed his by the handlebars. Then he leaned it back down and picked up a pebble. He kneeled by Tim's bike and let the air out of both tires. He jumped on his bike and pedaled away as fast as he could, swerving when he reached up to wipe away his tears.

Tim pulled the pillow off his face and stared at the ceiling. He cursed. And then he forced himself up. He pulled on his sneakers and climbed out the window. He slid off the roof and ran over to his bike to find the tires flat. He looked down the alley and started running as best he could.

When he felt dizzy and dried out in the tiny blinding sun, he doubled over with his hands on his knees and caught his breath. He walked through the alleys looking for Nicky. After about half an hour he found him, at the mouth of an alley, sitting against the back of a storage shed. The chain had fallen off his bike.

Nicky sat with his head tucked into his knees crying quiet with his body shaking. He didn't see Tim walk up. He didn't even know Tim was standing over him watching until Tim said his name soft and he looked up. The sun was so bright and Tim looked so sick and pale. It was like it wasn't even him.

"Nicky," Tim said. "What are you doing? I have been looking all over."

"So?" Nicky sniffed.

Tim felt stupid and ashamed. "So I don't know," he said. "So nothing."

"Yeah," Nicky said. "So nothing."

Tim didn't know what to say. Nicky had never looked at him like that before. How would he ever forget that look, he wondered. He walked over to Nicky's bike and turned it over onto its seat and handlebars. He threaded the chain back into place.

"I'm sorry," Tim said. "I'm sorry I hit you with the pillow. It's just. Like. I can't be perfect all the time just because you're scared of everything." It came out so wrong. Maybe he meant because he was, he thought.

Nicky glared at him. "The pillow? I don't care about the pillow! So what about the pillow? What about you promised? You don't even care that you promised."

"I know," Tim said. "I do. I really do. I'm sorry too for that. Nicky look at me. I'm really—"

"No you're not," Nicky said. "You don't care. Not really. You don't care about anything or this or that I lose the ticket and that I have to sit there with just the bad free apple and the plain milk. And you don't care." Nicky choked on a sob and gasped for air. "You don't care how they say I have the worst cursive when I'm not even doing anything. They just walk by and look down and say it. And say it's scribble scrabble. And they talk about my desk is messy when it isn't even really. It's just how my desks are. You don't even ever meet me before the buses anymore or want to go to to to—"

"Nicky," Tim said soft. "You don't understand."

"Yes I do so understand," Nicky said. "I understand better than you. You think just because you're smart you know everything when you don't even know the simplest things. I hope I never get as smart as you."

Nicky couldn't take it anymore. He couldn't take the pain of seeing Tim's face look like all the others' for another minute. He jumped up and grabbed his bike by the grips and flipped it back over. Tim stood in front of him and held tight to the handlebars. He felt like he was going to throw up and gulped a hard breath to keep it down.

Nicky pushed the handlebars toward Tim and pulled it back hard, wrenching it free from him.

"I'm sorry," Tim said.

"Go tell all your promises you're sorry," Nicky said. "Sorry for breaking them."

He pulled his bike towards him and threw his leg over the seat. Tim grabbed the handlebar and said don't.

"Let go," Nicky said.

Tim let go.

Nicky turned the bike around and started to pedal away. He looked back and saw Tim walking behind him and pedaled faster. Tim jogged to keep up. "Nicky just stop," he said.

Nicky stood on the pedals and pumped his legs to get away. Tim started to run after him, but Nicky pedaled faster, as fast as he could towards the end of the alley. "Nicky don't!" Tim called out, pleading.

Nicky kept pedaling fast but turned around to see if Tim was still there. Tim could see he was getting close to the end of the alley and the street. His voice called out loud and filled with worry. "Hey slow down! Nicky! Stop!"

Nicky heard the change in Tim's voice and looked forward to the end of the alley and the street. He slammed back on the pedals to brake. The chain clattered as it slipped off the flywheel.

Nicky slammed his chest as he fell into the handlebars. He swerved out of control and flew into the street. The car hit him at full speed.

Tim saw it hit and then vanish out of view of the alley as the tires screeched.

Everything stopped. Tim could hear only the rush of his own gasp and then he heard nothing but birds and his heartbeat and he saw the empty street and the start of the next alley across it. He screamed, "Nicky!" and he ran to the street.

He looked right and saw the car stopped in the middle of the street but he couldn't see Nicky. He screamed his name again. He heard the car door open and watched the driver get out in slow motion and disappear as he lowered himself to look beneath the car. The open door warning chimed. Tim screamed for Nicky again.

Tim sprinted to the passenger side of the car in the street and threw himself to the pavement. He looked under and stared right into Nicky's blank scared face, cheeks still streaked with tears. He was laying on his stomach under the middle of the car and his bike was bent and wedged beneath the rear wheels.

Nicky looked at Tim with his eyes wide open. There were little cuts on his forehead and his chin was scraped. His arm reached out as if for Tim. Tim grabbed his hand and he knew. He was dead.

"Nicky?" Tim asked anyway. "Nicky don't move. Don't move. I'm right here. I'm right here. Don't move. I'm not going anywhere."

Still holding Nicky's hand, Tim rolled on his back in the street and screamed, "Help! We need help!" Then softer he said, "Somebody please. Somebody please help us."

He turned and looked back at Nicky's face and held his hand and whispered his name, over and over, as the driver's feet walked away.

21

The days after were a blur. Mick didn't come back for the funeral. It rained. Nora couldn't bring herself to look at Tim. It was as if God had reached into her chest and pulled out the light in her heart, the goodness in her soul and told her no. Not you. You don't get to have this.

In the car driving home in the rain, she smoked with the windows rolled up and Tim felt like he couldn't breathe. He followed her into the house in his thrift store dress shirt and pants that itched and a clip on tie. He watched her pull a chair over to the cabinets. She climbed it and reached to the top, near the ceiling. She pulled down a full bottle of vodka. She was crumbling inside. She didn't talk to him or look at him as she climbed down. She twisted off the cap and dropped it on the floor, walked into the bedroom and slammed the door behind her.

Tim climbed the stairs slow as gallows and when he got to the room they had shared it was like somebody else had lived there. Nothing made sense. Things he owned all his life looked strange now. Books he had read, read to Nicky even, now looked like they were written in some strange language. The toys they had once loved and played with together looked broken and shabby and thrown away by strangers.

He yanked the clip-on tie off and threw it. He pulled open the shirt, tearing the buttons as he wrestled himself out of it. He tried to rip it more but couldn't. He dropped it to the floor and pulled down the awful pants that smelled wet from the rain and stuck to his legs as he tugged them over his sneakers and then kicked them off too. He stood in the room, a stranger to himself and everything in it. He wondered how this could even be him. He turned to ask Nicky.

———

KATHLEEN HELD ON FOR A COUPLE MORE MONTHS, BUT THAT HAD been her last chemo appointment. At that point, she and the doctor agreed, it was just hurting. It was stage four. It had spread. It was time to focus on managing the pain. Towards the very end she told James, "Don't you worry about me. I know where I'm going. But you take care of our babies for me."

She knew, she told him, he could do it. "You're stronger than you know, James Sullivan," she told him. But when she was gone, he fell apart.

Cara would wake and dress Katy. She would drive her to school early for the free breakfast before driving herself to school. Some mornings they would have to step over him on the living room floor. At work they said they understood, they really did. Maybe he should take a few days. When he didn't go back, they fired him. His manager said there was nothing he could do. He got another job and got fired again within a couple weeks. He didn't sleep and in the mornings he poured vodka into his coffee. Sometimes he didn't even pour the coffee. Cara hid the car keys.

And one night, late, after school and after work and after

making Katy dinner and getting her to bed and then studying she found him face down on the kitchen table. She went to the bathroom and stared at herself in the mirror, with her pastel sweater and her gold name necklace and her cheerleader hair. She didn't even know her. She went back to the kitchen and got the big scissors from the junk drawer. James hadn't moved.

She took the scissors to the bathroom and stared in the mirror. She grabbed fistfuls of her hair and cut it off in long thick chunks until it lay around her in piles in the sink and the toilet and the floor, until it was all off and her hair was cropped and crooked and patchy. She walked back to her room, quiet to not wake Katy, and yanked all her little nice girl clothes off their hangers and threw them on the floor. She didn't want to be her anymore. She wanted to be another girl. Someone who could get out of there. Someone who would leave. No matter what.

22

While the spaghetti boiled, James looked at the calendar and counted the days until Cara left for school. He warmed the sauce in a pan and strained the spaghetti. He fixed two bowls and put extra grated cheese on Katy's. He carried them to the couch and put them on the TV trays and sat next to her. He looked over. "Did you drink all your lemonade already?" he asked. He got up and poured her some more.

He put the glass on her tray and sat down. She twirled her fork into the spaghetti as James pointed the remote to the TV and clicked it on. One Day at a Time was just starting. They both loved that show. The single mother raising her two daughters.

James tucked his fork into his spaghetti but froze when the theme song started. He had watched enough to know the lyrics, but he felt like he was hearing them for the first time. This is it! This is it! This is life!

He sat forward a little. This is it! This is it! This is your life. This is it! Hold on tight. You don't need to be sure. Get up on your feet. Don't worry. Just take it as it comes. Just take it one day at a time. One day at a time. One day at a time.

He felt something in his chest, some feeling he didn't recognize, like something breaking and melting at the same time. He sniffed hard. He thought of the placards in the church basements. All of a sudden it all seemed so simple. So possible. Just today. Just do it today. Katy looked over at him and saw the tears streaming down his face.

"Daddy?" Katy asked. "Why are you crying? Do you miss mommy?"

James wiped his eyes but the tears kept coming. He pulled Katy closer. "Oh Beans," he said. "I always miss mommy. But I'm not sad. I'm just tired."

"You never get tired anymore," Katy said. She leaned into him. "Not like you used to. Not right in the daytime."

He kissed the top of her head. They watched the episode. It was funny. During the commercials he cleared their trays and came back with a bowl of ice cream for Katy.

They watched part of another show, then Katy yawned and rested her head on James. Her eyes looked heavy. He stood and picked her up and held her to his chest as he carried her to her bedroom. She rested her head on his shoulder with her eyes closed, breathing soft.

James held her in one arm while he turned down her blanket, then rested her into bed. She opened one eye and pursed her lips not to smile. "You little pretender," he said. "You're awake."

Katy opened her eyes and James sat on the edge of her bed.

"Daddy," she asked. "Did you learn the words?"

"Beans," he said.

"Did you look at the record?" she asked.

"The one with the old man?" James asked. "That looks like me?"

"You do not," she said. "But did you?"

James sighed. "Yes," he said.

"Did you listen?" Katy asked.

"Honey," he said. "I'm not a singer."

"Everybody is," she said. "Will you?"

James looked into Katy's eyes and she looked back into his. She raised her eyebrows and he had to laugh. "Okay okay," he said. "Move over."

James propped up a pillow and laid down next to her. She slid closer and nestled into her father. He cleared his throat and looked at the ceiling. Katy raised her head and looked at him. "Now's good," she said.

James took a breath and sighed. Katy laid back down and closed her eyes. She placed her arm across his stomach and James sang to her in a slow soft hush.

"Yesterday," he started and got embarrassed.

With her eyes closed, Katy whispered, "You can do it."

He looked down at Katy, breathing soft with her eyes closed. She pulled herself closer. He remembered the words he had copied into his notebook late the night before at the kitchen table, reading the lyrics off the record sleeve. And as best as he could, he sang Katy the Cara song about yesterday, when he got so old he thought that he might die, so old it made him want to cry, and how he felt as cold and scared as a child, without her, without her, without her.

Near the end, he felt a lump in his throat and he stopped. Katy lay quiet, asleep. He stayed still next to her and followed his breath as it opened like dove wings behind his heart. And he looked for the tightness he had felt since he was a boy. The fear and doubt and shame that coiled inside him, and made him always feel different and separate and alone. He looked in his chest and he looked behind his eyes and he looked across his shoulders and he looked in the pit of his stomach, but he couldn't find it anywhere. It had been lifted.

23

Cara didn't know New Miltown, so she drove slow down side streets with Tim's address written on the flyer on the seat beside her. The houses got smaller, and the chain link appeared like cages between the streets and the small lawns littered with rain faded toys.

She looked up and saw the street name on a sign that leaned like it had been hit. She turned and drove slow with her windows open, the radio volume low on the station from the school she would be going to soon. She found the house.

She parked outside and looked at the numbers on the black plastic mailbox, and then the same numbers in her handwriting on the flyer. This was it. She considered for a minute slipping it back into drive and u-turning from the curb. But something wouldn't let her. Her heart racing, she got out of the car and walked toward the front porch.

Inside, Nora looked out the kitchen window at this strange fairy creature coming closer, floating towards her, disappearing to her porch now. She walked to the front door and pulled it open before Cara could ring the doorbell.

Cara was reaching for the button when the door opened and

she again came face to face with Nora's wasted faded beauty. She looked haunted. The menacing glamor, the eerie leopard print allure that charged the air around her in the supermarket was gone. She looked strung out and exhausted, with a mad baffled sadness she cast like a shadow.

Behind Cara, a cloud covered the sun as Nora stepped out onto the porch like an eclipse. She eyed Cara with suspicion, the intensity of her energy forcing Cara back a half step.

"I know you," Nora said. "How do I know you?"

Cara lost her words in Nora's eyes for a moment. "I work at the Stop and Shop," she said. "From the other night?"

"Oh," Nora said, like a koan. "Is that how we know each other?"

Cara looked past Nora, nervous and not sure what she was seeing behind her. Nora leaned forward and then trained her eyes back on Cara's face. Cara waited for her to ask what she wanted, why she was there.

The air around Nora felt thin like she had changed the elevation. Cara took another breath. "Is Tim here?" she asked.

"Yes," Nora said. "He is here."

Nora stood there for a moment, gathering some frayed threads of courage, before stepping backwards into the house, leaving the door open behind her. Cara stepped in.

Nora walked the path to the kitchen and then turned and looked back at Cara and watched her try to take it all in. Nora exhaled and looked at the tough delicate girl. She wanted to say something. She wanted to explain or warn her.

"It happens so fast," Nora said. "Everything takes forever and it happens so fast."

Cara nodded. She understood. She remembered the stages of her mother's cancer. That's how the end felt.

Nora pointed to the stairs. She said, "Up there. If you hit the stars you went too far."

Cara slipped through the wreckage piled higher than her eyes and climbed the stairs to Tim's room.

Tim lay on his back on his bed, staring at the water-stained ceiling, thinking of his wrists after he punched the windows. The rivulets of blood dripping down his fingers as he moved his hand in wonder, how he couldn't even feel it, how it was easy.

The doorknob turned and he shot up and said, "No," and then louder, "I said no." The door opened slow and from the darkness below, Cara stepped in.

The room was bright from the late afternoon summer sun. Cara blinked and then found him, sitting up on his bed, stunned.

"Can I come in?" she asked.

Tim nodded slow. "How are you here?" he asked.

"I don't know," she said. "I just. I called information. You said you walked from here. You spelled your name, remember? Like mess up without the m?"

"Nobody comes here," he said.

Cara stepped forward and cocked her head, looking at his eye. "Are you okay?" she asked.

"Yeah," he said. "Now."

Cara circled the sparse room, then sat next to him on the bed. She brought her knees to her chest and turned to him. They looked into each other's eyes, shy, and then Cara said, "Do you want to get out of here?"

"Yes," Tim said. "More than anything."

They stood together and Cara turned toward the door.

"Oh," Tim said. "Let's like." He pushed the door shut and he led her to the open window.

They walked around to the front of the house and got into her car. Cara started the engine. Tim looked back. He could see a trace of Nora's pale face in the dark kitchen window as they pulled away.

CARA STOLE GLANCES OF TIM'S KIND SAD EYES, CATCHING glimpses of the black eye when he looked over at her. "I can't believe it's me and you," she said. "Where should we go? What should we do?"

"Anywhere," Tim said. "Nowhere. Anything. Nothing."

She looked over and smiled at him. "That sounds perfect."

Tim rode with the orange and red sunlight warm on his face, squinting and smiling, his heart waking. Close to flying.

Cara smiled at him again and then said, "Oh let's play cassette roulette. You go." She opened the center console between them where she threw her tapes. "Close your eyes."

Tim smiled and closed his eyes and clattered the tapes together as he picked one.

Cara said, "Don't look. Watch I'm gonna mortify myself."

With his eyes closed, he felt her hand on his as she took the cassette he had picked. She looked at it.

"That's a good one," she said. She popped it into the tape player and turned up the volume. Tim listened excited and nervous to the soft hiss of the tape winding.

The drum roll thundered and jarred Tim stiff with shock as the big guitars of Refugee kicked in, flooding his mouth with the sickening sweetness of maraschino cherry and his nose with the sting of cigarette smoke and his eyes with the nightmare visions of his father's mangled face on the floor of the bar.

He lurched forward and punched eject. The white noise of radio static hissed around them. Cara looked over startled at Tim's red shaken face.

He swallowed hard, terrified he had ruined everything. He couldn't help it. He didn't know how to explain. "I'm sorry," he said. "I just. I fucking hate that song."

"What?" Cara said. She lowered the volume of the static. She pulled to the side of the road and turned to look at him, her eyes full of kindness. "Nobody doesn't like Tom Petty."

Tim couldn't look at her. "I do," he said. "Or don't I mean? I just." He shrugged, the words lost.

Cara hushed him and said, "Trust me?"

Tim looked at her. He nodded.

Cara pushed the cassette back into the player and hit fast forward quick. The tape chirped as it skipped the song. When it stopped at the end, Cara pressed fast forward again. It skipped through another song and then fluttered in silence before the next one started.

The car filled with garbled clattering drums that sounded like they were being played backwards somehow and fast strummed rustles of hollow acoustic guitar. It sounded like the tape was breaking.

"Oh is it eating it?" Tim asked.

Cara looked over and shook her head and smiled and said, in perfect time with a voice on the tape, "It's just the normal noises in here." She laughed out loud and the car filled with a beautiful jangle of electric guitars and the drums went off like fireworks. Cara reached over and turned it way up just as the vocals started.

She pulled back onto the road and drove faster and the wind blew through the open windows and the chorus rang out like a rhapsody. She turned and lip-synced it to him like she was whispering a secret. *Baby even the losers get lucky sometimes.*

24

Cara pulled down a long gravel road and drove until she reached a chain stretched across it. They got out of the car and Tim followed her as she stepped over. They walked together down a path worn through tall trees.

"It looks like nowhere," Cara said. "But I don't live too far from here. I used to walk down here all the time. When my dad was drinking."

Tim stopped walking and looked at her. "Oh, wait," he said. "The other day? You meant he was at a meeting meeting, didn't you? Like a AA meeting. Not a business meeting."

Cara nodded. They kept walking.

"Wow, yeah," Tim said. "At that church there. They made me go to those for a while."

"What do you mean, made you?" Cara asked. "Who they?"

Tim let out a long slow breath. "I don't know," he shrugged. "After." He looked over at her. "After my little brother died. He got hit by a car. And. Cause. Cause after I wouldn't talk ever. Cause I was having nightmares. Cause I saw it happen. And then I kept seeing it, all the time. Every time I got to a corner. Every time a car passed. And then when I wouldn't answer in class, I got detention and I punched out all the window panes and cut my hand all up and got blood all everywhere. So the school made these doctor appointments for me but my mom kept missing them. And then I like heard the Ramones for the first time and about sniffing glue." He shrugged and shook his head. "So I started doing that. But it was really bad and it gave me these headaches all the time and I started not remembering anything, so I started stealing booze instead to stop but I like had to break into people's houses to get it?"

"You broke into people's houses?" Cara asked.

"Yeah," he said, looking down. "I'd just walk in. Most people, it's almost like nothing bad ever happens so they don't even think to lock their doors. All the houses were so clean. There was a place for everything. But, anyway. I got caught. Of course. Cause I kept going back to this pastor's house, over by that church there. Because he was never home and he had the biggest liquor cabinet. And then one night he was just sitting at the table in the dark, waiting for me. He was really nice actually. He said if I went to the meetings they had there he wouldn't call the police on me. So, yeah, that's who they."

"Did it work?" Cara asked.

"No," Tim said. "Well, yeah. I don't know. For a while. The people were nice. I liked the stories. I liked having someplace to go. And there was coffee for free. But then, like, one night I was sitting there before it started and some old like old timer AA guy came up to me and was like, How old are you even? And I go, like, fifteen or whatever. And the guy just laughed at me. He was like, What the hell are you doing here? You look like you got years of fucking up ahead of you. So I was just like, fuck you too, and stopped going."

"Wow," Cara said. "What an asshole."

"Yeah," Tim said. "But whatever. It was nice of that pastor though anyway. He came and checked on me a couple times but I didn't answer the door. I don't do anything anymore really. I just, I don't know. I, like, go to the library?"

Cara gave him a skeptical look and he laughed. "Really," he said. "Pretty punk huh?"

Cara smiled. "So punk."

They walked together in silence. "Why did you tell me all that?" Cara asked.

"I don't know even," Tim said. But he was glad he had. "I guess maybe I wouldn't mind if you knew. I mean like. I wouldn't mind if you knew me."

Cara looked at him and smiled with her eyes. "You punched out all the windows in detention?" she asked.

Tim stopped walking and held out his right wrist to show her the constellation of scars. She touched them with her fingertip. "You get that from Catcher in the Rye?" she asked and smiled.

"How did you *know?*" Tim laughed. "You gotta stop doing that."

"I told you I was on to you," she said.

Cara held his hand as they walked the rest of the path, stepping over the empty beer bottles and cigarette packs that appeared. The path ended at the edge of a vast empty abandoned limestone quarry.

They stood together at the edge and looked over. The dry rocky bottom was littered with some empty beer cans and wine bottles and trash. The walls were spray painted with graffiti initials.

"I used to come here more," Cara said. "Like all the time. When it was still full. My dad would be so crazy, like blackout crazy, screaming at people who weren't even there, crying, breaking shit. My mom would get Katy and lock herself in her room and I'd just sneak out and come down here. It was so pretty at night. So quiet. When it was a full moon you could see the reflection on the water and I'd just stare at it and pretend it fell out of the sky and sank down to the bottom."

Tim leaned over the edge and looked down. "It's far," he said.

"Yeah it was really deep," Cara said. "It was nice. But then I think something bad happened, because I came one day and there were all these guys in orange jackets with trucks, lowering these big blue pumps in and they drained all the water out, emptied it dry. I don't really come here as much now. But it used to be my favorite place."

"Really?" Tim said. "It's still, I don't know. It's still kinda cool."

"Yeah, it's okay," she said. "I wish you could have seen it like it was before it got all trashed though. It was so pretty."

Cara took Tim's hand, and they laced their fingers together and stood with their feet on the edge of the abyss. Cara stepped back but Tim stayed. He closed his eyes and put his arms out. He took a breath and took a big step back. He exhaled. He looked over and smiled at Cara. He rolled his eyes at himself and shook his head.

"I don't usually like heights," he said.

"Are you afraid you'll fall?" she asked.

"I'm more afraid I'll jump I think," he said.

Tim walked back from the edge and sat down. Cara sat next to him and wrote his name in the dirt in front of him with her finger and then drew an arrow pointing to him. She wrote the word Me in front of herself. He turned to her and they looked in each other's eyes, the hint of a kiss in the air like lilac.

"When did your brother die?" Cara asked. Her voice sounded soft and far away.

"Three years ago," he said.

"How old were you?"

"Fourteen," he said. "Wait, no, thirteen still."

"How old was he?" she asked.

"He was ten," Tim said.

"Oh my god," Cara said. "Were you close?"

Tim looked away, across the empty quarry. He nodded.

"What was his name?" Cara asked.

"Nicholas," Tim said. "But Nicky. I always called him Nicky."

Tim turned back and looked at Cara, his eyes wet with memories.

"Oh, you know what?" Cara said. "I'm sorry. I just, wanted to know. But you don't have to."

"No, no it's okay," Tim said. "It's good. I used to be so afraid that time would pass and I would start to forget things, all the little best things about him. And then that's when he'd be really gone. When he'd really be dead. When I, if I, forgot him."

A tear rolled down Tim's cheek. He wiped it away. "Shit," he said. "Sorry. So when I couldn't sleep I would just think of everything about him that I could, every littlest thing, and repeat it over and over in my head, to memorize him. So I could keep him with me."

He looked at the sky, remembering Nicky.

"God," he said. "What was Nicky like? Everything he was he was like the opposite at the same time. It was funny. Like, he was tough and like super sensitive too. His first day of first grade at lunch, I wasn't there cause I was in fourth then, I had the second lunch. And these three third graders cut in front of him in line and tried to take his chocolate milk and make him have one of their like skim milks instead and he just started swinging."

Tim laughed soft. "Right there in the cafeteria line. It was so tough. But then when we walked home when he told me he just cried and cried. He cried cause he hit 'em and felt sorry for it. And he cried cause they were mean to him, and cried cause they didn't like him and cried cause he got in trouble on his first day. He always would lose his lunch ticket after that though. You like bought the ticket in the morning and then gave it to the lunch ladies to pay for the lunch. And he lost his like every day. He saved everything. He thought every scrap of paper was special. He had so much stuff in his desk at school. He'd put the ticket in his desk and then couldn't find it. So they'd send him down to me, to my class. And I'd give him mine so he could eat lunch, and I'd ask him how his day was going and like, tell him everything was okay and what we'd do later."

They sat quiet for a few moments, and then Tim continued. "School scared him. He was really smart. He could know the words to any song after listening to it just once. But, I don't know. He had a hard time with reading, with like concentrating. I think, maybe, he might have been dyslexic maybe. Something. He'd get so frustrated in school and all lost trying to keep up and he'd have these panic, like, attacks. He'd start breathing really fast and his voice would get all tight. He felt stuff really hard, and he worried a lot. I don't know." Tim stopped and looked at Cara. "This is kinda? I don't ever talk about this."

"I'm sorry," Cara said.

Tim sat silent for a moment. "And oh he liked the worst songs." Tim laughed. "Like REO Speedwagon and Journey and like any sappy radio song. He just loved them. He thought they were so pretty."

Tim shrugged. "Anyways. He was just him. There was nobody like him. He was just so—"

Cara sobbed, loud, sharp, sudden. It startled him. She looked over at him, her eyes raining tears. "My mom died."

"Your mom did?" Tim said, shocked. "Oh my god. I'm so sorry. When?"

"Around the same time as your brother I guess," she said. "Like three years ago."

Cara broke down crying, her face pressed into her bent knees and her shoulders heaving. She looked up, into Tim's eyes, her face flooded with tears. "My mom died," she said.

Tim sat in stillness and silence. Cara's pain poured out in torrents like a waterfall. He put his arm around her hunched shoulders and pulled her closer. He held her tight as she shook with tears. She pushed herself into him and cried until she stopped. She lifted her face from her knees and looked at Tim, wiping her tears away.

"I never cried after," she said. "I did when she was sick, all the time. And she'd tell me there was plenty of time for crying later. But when she died, I couldn't. Or I was scared to. Scared I wouldn't stop. And there was Katy. My little shadow. And my dad was all fucked up. Just falling down, just useless. And there wasn't plenty of time for crying. Not for me anyway. There wasn't any time at all."

Cara turned in the dirt to face Tim. She reached over and traced his face soft with her fingertip. She circled his eyes, down the bridge of his nose, across his lips. She traced up from his chin, along his jaw line and pushed his hair behind his ear. They leaned closer.

"Can I show you something?" she asked. Tim nodded. Cara stood and held out her hand to him. He took it and stood with her. "It's just over there," she said. "I want to show you my tree."

Cara held his hand and led him away from the quarry and off the path into the woods. She stopped at a lone tall white birch that seemed to glow in a dark grove of cypress. "Over here," she said, and stepped to the other side of the birch trunk.

Inside a plastic ziplock bag, duct taped shut around its edges like a gray frame, was her mother's funeral book. Cara had nailed it into the tree, and then wrapped wire around the nails to secure it.

Tim stepped closer and looked at the photo of Kathleen, young and smiling, on the cover. Underneath her photo, it read, "Kathleen Sullivan, devoted wife and mother. 1947-1984." Beneath that, there was an Irish proverb.

Tim read it out loud. "Death leaves a heartache no one can heal. Love leaves a memory no one can steal."

"That's my mom," Cara said. "I thought if I sealed it up really careful, and nailed it there, that maybe it would grow right into the tree and she could be there, right there, forever."

Tim looked at Cara, aching to kiss her. Cara stared into his eyes and longed to kiss him too. She looked away.

"It's gonna be so weird to not be able to just walk down here and talk to her whenever I need to," she said. She looked back at Tim. "After I leave next week."

Tim looked at the funeral book against the white paper bark of the birch tree and realized what she just said. He turned to her. "When you what?" he asked.

Cara stood quiet. "When I leave," she said. "For school."

"For school?" he asked, confused.

"For college," she said. "I'm going in like a week." She saw his face fall. "A little more. Aren't you?" she asked, knowing the truth but not wanting to know. "You said you were done. You said you skipped."

Tim stood dazed and didn't answer. He looked up. "What? No. I mean, yeah, I did. I finished. But I'm not." He shook his head. "College? No. I'm not going." His voice hardened a bit. "I'm not going anywhere."

"But why not?" she asked.

"What do you mean why not?" he said. "Because like look at me. Why not. Why like, how could I even?" He shook his head.

A hint of anger crept into Cara's voice. "Look at you?" she

asked. "What does that even mean? I am looking at you. I'm looking right at you."

Tim looked down. "I don't have any money or anything."

"Money?" Cara asked, the word sour in her mouth. "Who has money? You just get some job and save it up. That's why I work all the time. Every day after school, all summer. To get out of here."

"Well great," Tim said. "Good. I didn't do that though. I wouldn't even know how to leave even."

Cara stared at him, not letting him slip out. "You do too know," she said. "I bet you leave every night in your head. If it was just about knowing how, you would have already figured it out."

Tim shrugged, his heart breaking. "I don't know."

"Don't you?" she asked. "What's here for you?"

He looked back at her. "Nothing."

"So you do know," she said.

Cara stepped closer to him, but he backed up. She stepped again and he felt himself press against the birch tree. She took another step and her body was almost touching his. She looked into his eyes.

"Will you kiss me now?" she asked.

Tim shook his head. "Why?" he asked.

"Because I want you to kiss me," she said. "I wanted you to kiss me the second you walked up to me and said you were looking for a friend."

"You're just gonna be gone though," he said.

"So?" she asked. "So's everything. But I'm right here now, aren't I? Aren't we?"

Tim breathed her in and exhaled, "Yes."

"So kiss me," she whispered. "Now is all there ever even is."

Cara balled the front of his shirt in both of her fists and pulled herself to him. Tim looked into her closed eyes for a moment, hesitating. Then he closed his eyes and fell forward into the space between them.

They kissed. Leaning against the birch tree. They kissed. Pressed against each other. They kissed. Tender, passionate, innocent, desperate. They kissed. As the sky grew deeper blue and the stars shined through them. They kissed. For the first and last time.

25

Cara pulled to the curb. Tim looked at the dark scowl of the house. Cara put the car in park and looked over. Tim turned from the passenger window and looked back at her.

"I still have a week almost," she said. "And I'm done with work, so I have more time."

Tim nodded and tried to smile at her.

"You look so sad," she said.

"Some things are sad."

Cara nodded. Tim looked at her, watching her see him. He slipped her face into his heart like he was pressing a wildflower between the pages of a paperback. He got out of the car and closed the door quiet behind him. He bent down to the open window.

"Goodnight, Tim," she said.

He looked at her one last time. "Goodbye Cara."

He walked to the dark porch. He didn't turn when he heard her pull away.

Inside, he looked across the suffocating wreckage and saw Nora asleep on the couch. Her records were scattered on the floor around her, along with photos and some paperbacks. He walked over and checked on her. She lay on her side, taking slow, soft, shallow breaths. He pulled the blanket up to her shoulders to cover her. There wasn't much else he could do.

He climbed the stairs slow and stopped at the door of his room. It was half open, the light on inside. He thought he had closed it. He always closed it.

He walked into the room and saw a cardboard box folded shut in the middle of his floor. He sat and opened it. It was full of old greeting cards. Birthday cards, Easter cards, Christmas cards, good luck cards, special occasion cards. They were all for Nicky, from Nora. He must have saved them all.

Tim lifted one to read it. On the front was a cartoon Mad Hatter in green. The caption read, "I'd Have to be Mad as a Hatter to Forget..." Tim opened the card. Inside, it said, "Your birthday!" Next to it, Nora had written, "Save this for something special!" There was a twenty dollar bill inside.

Tim set the card to the side of the box and opened more. There were cards for other birthdays, and half birthdays. There were cards that said happy summer, and happy first day. On one of the special occasion cards, Nora had written, "I knew you could do it."

Every card had cash in it. Tens and twenties and fives and ones. The bills fell into his lap when he opened them. He read them all, setting them in a neat pile next to the box and putting the cash to the side. Under all the cards, he found Nicky's dented metal lunchbox. Nora had gotten it for him after Tim went to high school, after she started making him lunch from home to take. On the front, it read, "Wild Frontier" with a drawing of a cowboy riding his horse away from a line of wagons and a campfire.

Tim lifted the lunchbox into his lap and opened the metal lid. It was filled with Nicky's old lunch tickets, the ones he said he'd lost in order to come see Tim. There must have been a hundred. He held one up and stared at it. He dropped it back into the lunchbox and ran his fingers through them.

At the very bottom, he found a small, wallet-size photo face down. On the back, in careful letters, Nicky had printed "My Brother." The h and the last r were backwards. Tim flipped it over. It was an old school portrait of him, just like the picture of Nicky he kept under his speaker. Same sky blue backdrop, same crooked smile, same cowlicks, same sad eyes.

Tim put the tickets and the picture back in the lunchbox. He placed the lunchbox back in the cardboard box and put all the greeting cards on top of it. Sitting up on his knees, he gathered the cash in a neat pile and folded it without counting it. He slipped the money into his front pocket.

He crossed the room and tilted back the speaker. He picked up the picture of Nicky and put it in his other pocket. He turned out the light and climbed out his window.

Tim slid down the roof and walked alone down the alley, not sure where he should go, or what he should do. He walked down Main Street but everything was dark and closed. He didn't see the bus lights approaching him from behind.

Just as he got to the bus stop, he heard a great hush of air, as if something huge was trying to quiet him. He jumped a little startled and looked over at the towering coach of the Bonanza bus.

The door opened. Surprised, he looked inside. The driver nodded and Tim nodded back. The driver looked at him from behind the wheel and waited.

"Well," the driver said. "You coming?"

"Oh," Tim said, understanding. "Where are you going?"

"All the way to the city," the driver said. "But you can go anywhere from there. It's all somewhere till you get there."

"That's true," Tim said. He put his hand in his pocket and felt the folded bills. "How much to go the whole way?"

"Ah, don't worry about it," the driver said. "I hate driving it empty."

"Yeah?" Tim said.

"Yeah," the driver said. "It always seems to take so much longer when you're alone."

The driver looked at Tim. "You coming?"

"Yeah," Tim said. "I am." He stepped into the bus and climbed to a seat in the first row, across from the driver.

The driver pulled the door closed and the interior lights dimmed. He looked up in the mirror at Tim and smiled. "It's funny," he said. "Nobody ever gets on here."

He shifted into gear. "You ready?" he asked.

Tim nodded. "I am ready."

"You look ready," the driver said. He looked at his watch. "Right on time."

The driver let out the clutch and pulled away. Tim watched the town go by out the tall front windshield. As they passed the end of the sidewalk, and then Buddy's, the driver stepped on the gas. The needle of the speedometer climbed to fifty-five. Tim leaned forward in his seat and watched the bright headlights shine into the darkness ahead.